AN
Impossible
THING
TO SAY

AN
Impossible
THING
TO SAY

Arya Shahi

Allida

An Imprint of HarperCollinsPublishers

Library of Congress Cataloging-in-Publication Data

Names: Shahi, Arya, author.
Title: An impossible thing to say / by Arya Shahi.
Description: First edition. | New York : Allida, an imprint of HarperCollins
Publishers, 2023. | Audience: Ages 13 up. | Audience: Grades 10–12. | Summary:
In the aftermath of 9/11, high school sophomore Omid grapples with finding the
right words to connect with his grandfather, embrace his Iranian heritage, and
express his feelings towards a girl, until he immerses himself in the rhymes and
rhythms of rap music and finds his voice.
Identifiers: LCCN 2022058362 | ISBN 9780063248359 (hardcover)
Subjects: CYAC: Novels in verse. | Family life—Fiction. | Iranian Americans—
Fiction. | Rap (Music)—Fiction. | September 11 Terrorist Attacks, 2001—Fiction.
| LCGFT: Novels in verse.
Classification: LCC PZ7.5.S45 Im 2023 | DDC [Fic]—dc23
LC record available at https://lccn.loc.gov/2022058362

Typography by Jenna Stempel-Lobell
23 24 25 26 27 LBC 5 4 3 2 1

First Edition

For Parisa, Rebecca, and Jessica

July 4th, 2001

Tonight, I met two people
I've never met before,
from a country
I've never been to.

The Persians of Tucson, Arizona
(aka my relatives),
gathered at the gate
in the airport
in a state
we've never
felt before.

My whole family
was beside me
as my family
was made
whole.

Tonight, I met my grandparents.

Baba Joon and Maman Joon
stepped off the plane, stepped out of
the pictures in their frames,
and right into our lives.

Maman Joon cried
and held her two daughters tight, close
like kids, though they'd grown into women
since the last time she'd seen them.

Baba Joon smiled
and greeted us all, shaking hands,
kissing cheeks, making jokes in Farsi
about their terrible flight.

"We were delayed twenty years!"

Then he went to hold his daughters too,
and everyone was still laughing
as everyone started crying.

And just like that,
all my mom's stories,
about her childhood,
about her parents,
about her past,
caught up
to us.

In the back seat of our car,
I sat between my grandparents
as we drove home and thought

some part of them
is some part of me

and all those fireworks
far off in the sky
might as well
have been
for us.

July 4th, 2001, Part 2

When we got home
and everyone was getting ready for bed,
Baba Joon opened his beat-up briefcase
and handed me a present.

A small journal,
the size of a paperback,
bound in beautiful brown leather,
containing crisp cream pages
with gold-foiled edges.

The cover was embossed with a crest
of what looked like a dog/bird/lion
swinging its feathery tail
and wearing huge,
regal wings.

*"I hear you like to write.
This is for you, Omid jan."*

And then he switched to English
and slowly said,
"I love you."

"Merci. I love you too, Baba Joon."

A Hard Thing To Say

"I love you"
is a hard thing to say
when you mean it,
but you're also thinking,
"I don't know you."

Suitcases

Maman Joon and Baba Joon moved to America from Iran
and only brought two suitcases with them.

When Mom, Dad, Amir, and I went
on vacation to Hawaii last summer,
we took eight suitcases with us, and it still felt like
it wasn't enough, like something was missing,
like we had forgotten something important, back home.

It's how I've always felt.
Like I'm forgetting, or I'm disconnected from, something.
Like an island. Not like I'm *on* an island.
Like I *am* an island. Waiting to be discovered,
waiting to be claimed, waiting
to be a part of something, bigger.
Waiting to be familiar, with family.
Not just Amir, and Mom, and Dad, but the people
and the place we came from,
the history we once had
a hold on.

I've always wanted a history I could handle,
not just hear about.

Maman Joon and Baba Joon moved to America,
their whole lives packed into two taped-up suitcases.
Which must have been hard,
but makes me happy.

Because we're fast approaching familiar.
Heading toward the handling.

We're on our way to wonderful,
and I didn't even have to pack.

Home

Iran was always home.
Until it wasn't.

Iran was always whole.
Until it wasn't.

Apparently, Iran used to be really different.
(I've lost count of how many times my mom has told me,
"Tehran was the Paris of the Middle East.")

There was a revolution in Iran in 1979,
and my parents both left right before that.
But their parents stayed behind.

Which sounds harsh now,
but maybe it wasn't then?

My parents met in the States,
then dated in the States,
then married in the States.

In Iran, my parents might have never met,
might have never dated, and definitely
would have never married.

It's against the law there for a Muslim to marry a Bahá'í.

(It's against the law for a Muslim
to *anything* a Bahá'í, really . . .
except kill? I mean, I don't really know.
I'm pretty sure it's illegal to even be a Bahá'í in Iran.

7

But I don't want to ask Mom.
Enough of her relatives
have died
that it's too embarrassing to admit to her
that I still don't quite understand why.)

Mom's family is Bahá'í,
Dad's family is Muslim,
but that's easy to forget,
because our family is lucky.

Dad hasn't ever seemed to care about the "politics" of it.
I asked him once: How is all that even possible?
How can a belief
be illegal?

He shrugged, at first. Then he explained it like this:

All the religions of the world
seem to be waiting around
for some guy to come back
and save us or take us
to a better place.

Bahá'ís believe that guy already came,
pretty recently, actually, and told us
that all the prophets of the past were right,
but that it was time for us to come together
and follow *him*, to move forward as one.

When Muslims took over Iran
in 1979, they made their church the state.
Claimed *their* God was calling all the shots.

8

They gave God a say in everything
from speeding tickets
to executions.

But if the Bahá'í prophet and his believers were right,
that would mean all those Muslims were listening
to the wrong God.

A false God — overseeing absolutely everything.
Could you imagine?
How quickly a country built on false beliefs
could crumble?

The folks in charge had to keep that from happening . . .
So they started silencing the Bahá'í crowd real quick.

Long Distance

We still have family in Iran.
Mostly Dad's.
Most of Mom's got out.

I was born here.

When my parents call Iran to talk to their relatives,
I listen. I try to keep track of all the names,
imagining faces in my mind for each.

I can understand Farsi
much better than I can speak it.

Farsi is all about the vowels. Round sounds
that travel long distance with ease.

Mom speaks swift and smooth.
Like language was something no one ever struggled to learn.

Dad speaks loudly whenever he speaks,
but especially when he's on the phone with Iran.

Like he can't trust the microphone to do its only job.

I Keep Thinking How Lucky We Are To Be Americans

because the revolution in America happened so long ago
that the ground has stopped shaking.

We can try to build something nice here,
without worrying about the country
falling right back down.

When Muslims took over Iran,
they killed Baba Joon's sister.
She was Bahá'í.
So they hung her.

That was right around the time
Maman Joon and Baba Joon sent
their two teen daughters
to live in the States.

A journal is a safe place for secrets,
so here's mine:

I'm glad they left.
Because if they hadn't,
I wouldn't exist.

Brothers

I'm sleeping with Amir in his room.
Because Mom and Dad are in my room.
Because Maman Joon and Baba Joon are in their room.

Amir's room
used to be mine.
Then it was ours.
Now it's his.

I moved out.
Just a few weeks ago.
Just down the hall
into the balconied bedroom
that used to be Mom's office.

She hasn't needed it lately.
She hasn't been showing listings
or holding open houses much. She's been busy
helping Dad with paperwork and hiring new staff
ever since he started building the new store.

So with Mom's real estate career on hold
and a perfectly good balcony barely being used . . .
it only made sense that I move in, right?

Mom and Dad didn't think so at first,
but I begged (Mom has a soft spot
for putting your heart into anything),
and I bartered (Dad's a tough negotiator, but I offered to help
move rugs into the new store) until they finally came around.
That's how the balconied bedroom became mine.

But tonight, I'm back in my old room,
trying to fall asleep in a sleeping bag on the floor.

The moonlight is glinting
off dozens of golden statues where my bed used to be.
Amir's trophies. Soccer. Basketball. Karate. Flag football.
There's probably a trophy for rock-paper-scissors
in there somewhere.

My little brother is good at everything.

If I'm being honest,
that's one of the reasons I asked for my own room. I wanted,
needed, to not be reminded of Amir's amazingness
every single day. I only have one more year before
he finishes the eighth grade,
and we're back together
in the same school.

I want to live in a world where
we aren't being constantly compared
by everyone, every day.

And maybe if we didn't sleep in the same room every night,
I could stop comparing us too.

The Only Real Real

Amir's been helping Mom
move Maman Joon and Baba Joon into their new house
while I've been helping Dad move his rugs
into the new store.

Correction: trying to help.
Turns out, Dad doesn't really need my help —
he just wanted me around the store more often.

Our new store is in the fancy part of Tucson
(next to my favorite gelato shop),
and it's really, really big.
So big it can fit a few thousand rugs inside
without smelling like wool, or dust, or mothballs,
without smelling like the old store.

The new store smells clean.
And looks clean too. Pristine, like the marble staircase
that leads from the showroom floor to Dad's office.
That marble is imported from Italy. Or Greece?
Somewhere far away, across an ocean,
which adds to the almost overwhelming sense
that this is a special place, more museum
than market. Upstairs is lit like a gallery,
with artificial light shining on tiny tapestries
hanging on the walls. Downstairs is lit naturally,
with sunlight flowing through the massive glass windows
on the side of the building.

I'm not strong enough to help move the big rugs
(most of the men moving those ones are in the military

when they're not working at my dad's store), but I can unroll
the smaller ones in the antique gallery
upstairs and out of the way.

I see the price tag on a 6x9
and it stops me for a second.

Fifty-five thousand dollars for the rug
I'm unrolling.
Why would anyone pay that much
for something they are supposed to walk all over?
And Dad is adamant about that, by the way.
He tells all his clients they need to feel comfortable
stepping on their rugs. It's what they were made for, after all.

I walk over to his office,
where he's washing his face
in his private bathroom,
and that's when it starts . . .
That feeling I get
                    when I have something to say
                                        but I don't know how.

When I want to express a thought or impulse or emotion,
but instead I can only stumble or stammer or sweat.
"*Baba* — how is the — what is the — most expensive rug —
you've ever sold?"

"*Eh!* Why do you ask this, *baba jan*?"

I want to say: I don't know, Dad. I just noticed
that the rugs you sell are kind of expensive
and I wonder how they got to be so intricate

so beautiful and do you know how long
they take to make and does that mean
we're rich or upper middle class and
does that make us important and
how much does it really matter
what we are?

But none of that comes out. Even if it did,
I don't think it would make much sense.

Instead, I try to squeeze all of it, the whole feeling,
into another one-sentence attempt.
"I was just wondering — I've never thought of all these rugs
as — real art. Do you?"
Dad dries his face with a towel,
taking a second to think.
"If a handmade rug is not a real art, then what is?"
"I mean, a Picasso painting is real art, right?
Like the ones that sell for millions of dollars."
"*Nah, baba*, the only real real
art is advertising." He laughs.
Dad is proud of his answer.
He says it like it's the solution
to the world's greatest problem.

My feeling fades. And even though I didn't say
exactly what I meant to say, I try to let myself be
relieved, if only for a moment.

Because I know the feeling will come back.
It always does.

Sammy

The pinker his polo,
the more likely his collar
is popped.

Sammy Hall and I have been best friends
for like four years. Since the sixth grade,
since we were in the same homeroom
and realized we were both gamers
and eventually became the first guys
at school to build competitive Pokémon decks.

(He played a fire deck, so I built a water deck,
so he built an electric deck, so I built a grass deck,
but I mean, who really keeps track of that stuff anymore?)

Now we're about to be sophomores,
and Sammy's more focused on building an outfit
for the first day of school than building a Pokémon deck.

"Oh shoot, I forgot his cash at home,"
Sammy's mom says with a sigh as she swings the car
into the parking lot at the mall.

"It's okay, Sharon.
You took care of Omid last week. We'll get this one."
My mom turns around from the front passenger seat
with a silver credit card in her hand.

I nab the card, then jump out of the car with Sammy.
We head toward our favorite store:

Abercrombie & Fitch.

Sammy is going to work here
as soon as he's sixteen, or so he says,
and what he says is usually what happens . . .

Seriously.

Like at school, at lunch, Sammy can just
make the world work . . . differently. Need a table?
Which one? Take your pick! Sammy's on it.
Craving an extra-tasty meal? Order with Sammy,
and you're offered only the best:
"Can I interest you in the special today, boys?
We're serving *beef au jus*."
Sammy smiles real wide. "Why, thank you, Gloria,
but that'll depend on what's in it."
Sammy is only eating "lean meats" these days,
gotta prep for preseason, but that's okay,
cuz Gloria (aka the lunch lady) will make
sure Sammy gets anything Sammy needs.
And I'll get that too. And lunch is glorious
and grand and easy and maybe I'll look
like Sammy one day if I only eat "lean meats"
and forget about everything delicious.
But Sammy's not always with me
when I order lunch at school.
And the lunch lady (aka Gloria)
doesn't ask me if I want the special.
And I definitely don't ask her what it is
because what if I don't know the fancy name
and then the lunch line builds up behind me
and I get stuck not knowing what to do?

So instead I just say, "Pasta, please,"
as quickly as I can, to get
the whole thing over with.

That's the difference between Sammy and me —
Sammy carries himself with confidence.

Sidenote:

That expression is weird when you think about it.

"Carry yourself with confidence."

It means you walk around
with your head held high,
pretty proud about life.
But doesn't it also mean
that you're *carrying something* around?
Like maybe some stronger part of you
is carrying some weaker part of you
from place to place?

Oh, and another difference between Sammy and me
is I don't think I'll be getting a job anytime soon.
Unless I want to? I don't think my parents would make me,
but getting paid to hang out with Sammy at Abercrombie
wouldn't be the worst.

I just wish I looked better in their clothes.

I decide to buy some camo cargo shorts.
The shorts here are pretty awesome,
but I don't really like the shirts.

I don't think they bulge
in the right places.

Is there something wrong with me?
Or is there something wrong with the shirts?
Maybe it's the shirts. Maybe that's why the guys
on the bags and billboards aren't wearing them.
They're all shirtless because the shirts are so uncomfortable.
Or maybe it's because they've got muscles, like Greek gods,
so taking off your shirt is probably less of a big deal
for them than it is for us chubby mortals.

Come to think of it . . .
Everything in Abercrombie has muscles.
Even the cologne smells like tropical fruit — with muscles.

Sammy is going to fit right in.

Testing Well

"I'm coming over. Bust out the books."
Sammy isn't giving me much say in the matter.
"Man, I really dunno if it's worth it."
"Of course it is. Drop this whole 'I'm just a normal guy'
act. You're not gonna convince me."
He hangs up. School hasn't started yet . . .
but Sammy is coming over to study.
Let me explain.

We go to Nova, a private school that prides itself on placement.
Placement on lists in newspapers that tell parents
what's best for their kids. These lists prioritize
high schools that have a high percentage
of seniors placed into Ivy Leagues
or awarded prestigious
scholarships.

That's the kind of placement people care about.
The kind that's awarded.

And if my two years as a seventh and eighth grader playing
soccer on the sixth-grade soccer team taught me anything,
it's that prime placement is a prize that's never awarded
without passing some kind of test.

When it comes to soccer tryouts, that test looks a lot like laps.
A test where everyone passes right by me, literally.
A test I keep running, even though it's crazy hard,
because my dad keeps telling me, "Everything gets easier, *baba*,
as long as you never quit."

When it comes to school,
that prime placement test looks a lot like — well — a test.
And those are the kind of tests where I pass everyone else,
easily and often. My teachers say I "test well,"
but there are no trophies or cheerleaders for testing well,
just a couple lousy letters on a report card.

Sammy doesn't "test well." He lives well.
I'd much rather have that.

But I guess Sammy is going to try harder on tests this year
(college is creeping closer, and he probably wants
to see his name on one of those lists),
cuz he's coming over to my place to study
for our fall semester placement exams.
Those tests are how the school decides which students can
take honors or AP courses. Sammy insists I'm gonna do well,
and he wants to know how I study.

But . . . I don't really study. I just remember stuff
from class better than most people. And for some reason,
I'm embarrassed to tell him that.
So in the twenty minutes it takes
for him to get from his house to mine,
I make flash cards for the first time in my life.

We sit on my balcony as I make a show of taking the cards out
of my backpack, like they've always been there.
"So what've you got for me today, Teach?"
"Yeah, yeah, okay. Today we're gonna go over
the eight parts of speech and the quadratic equation.
And then we're gonna play *FIFA*."
He laughs. "That's my guy."

New Victories

Our school's full and formal title is
Victoria Nova College Preparatory School.
"Victoria Nova" means "New Victory"
in a forgotten language.
Latin.
That's a class we took in middle school,
where we learned the old words hiding under the new ones,
where we learned the old stories hiding under the new ones.

Victoria Nova High School and Victoria Nova Middle School
are on opposite sides of the same parking lot.

Last year, I was a freshman
on this side of the street for the first time,
surrounded by new people and new stories
and new words, and I kept waiting
for some of those new victories,
for a new version of Omid,
to show up, and cover up
the old one.

But it never happened.
I still struggled
with saying something —
anything — I really meant,
or being seen as anything except
Sammy's sidekick or Amir's shy big brother.

This year, I'm a sophomore, and I'm starting to think
if I want things to change, I'm going to have to
do something about it.

Scared

Sometimes some things change
whether you want them to or not.

Take Sundays, for instance.
Sundays were never special. We never had a family ritual.
No church or brunch, just a bunch of time for
Amir and me to play video games or soccer
in the backyard, or read a book,
or sometimes do homework
before bed.

But Sundays are about to change.
Mom told us today, "Maman Joon and Baba Joon
have asked us all to come to their house
every Sunday for dinner."

A *mehmooni* with my grandparents. Every Sunday.
My stomach does a flip. I'm not quite sick,
but I do feel mixed. Excited, I think?
And just a bit
scared.

Sometimes I get scared
of the ordinary
of a dinner
of a party
of that feeling
of having
something
to say.

May-MOO-knee

A *mehmooni* is different
than a party or a gathering. With a party or gathering,
there are invitations, a request for your presence,
and attendance is, of course, optional.

But there are no invitations to a *mehmooni*. It just happens.
You find out it's happening from your mom or
your cousin or your sibling. And then you go.

You don't not go.

The whole event is centered around a meal.
And just as a meal usually has courses,
so does a *mehmooni*.

First course: Arrivals and kissing
Second course: Small talk, card games, and table setting
Third course: Finishing in the kitchen, grilling in the yard
Fourth course: Mealtime
Fifth course: Joke telling and dishwashing
Sixth course: The show, the tell, the song, the dance
Seventh course: The poetry and the prayer
Eighth course: Kissing and departures

And at some point,
many, many, many hours
after you arrive,
you head home, full
of food and family
and sometimes feeling

like you caught a glimpse
of a glimmer that goes way back,
in an unbroken line,
to something
holy.

Housewarming

The first thing I noticed was how small their new house was.
My grandparents' entire home was the size of my bedroom.
And it was overflowing
with people.

My parents, aunts, uncles, cousins,
parents' cousins, cousins of cousins, and my
no-word-for-how-they-are-related-to-you-in-English "cousins."

All sifting through the three sections of the house,
the living room, the bedroom, and the kitchen.
All speaking accented English, Farsi,
or some combination of the two,
as they made small talk

> "*Remember when you could just
>   drive through* Craycroft and Sunrise
>   *without sitting in construction for hours?*"

or bigger talk

> "*President Khatami is a small step in the right direction for Iran —* "
> "Are you joking? *He's with the ayatollahs.*
>   They are all the same — *damn them.*"

I was wandering, looking for Amir
(somehow we got separated),
when I ran into Baba Joon
sitting in the corner of the living room
with another man, about his age, whom I'd never met before.
They were playing backgammon.

I was sweaty, the housewarming getting too warm,
and I was tired, so I sat next to Baba Joon to watch him play.

I wanted to tell him how happy I was that he was here,
but I didn't know how, so I didn't say anything.
I just sat there, silent.

He put his hand on top of my head,
running his fingers through my hair.
I didn't mind it.
He studied the board.
I studied his face.
He was thinking hard and fast,
blending strategy with luck in each roll.
I didn't get the point of the game at first,
but as the two of them spoke Farsi
and rolled the dice
back and forth,
totally ignoring the party
around them,
I started to understand
the goal of backgammon
was to find your way home.

But Is This It?

Mom's sister from Phoenix,
Dad's brother from LA,
Mom's "cousin" from Oro Valley,
all the blood relatives
I barely know.

Is this home?
Is this whole?
Shouldn't family
make you feel
full? Or at least
familiar?

We used to see each other more often.

They all used to live in Tucson.
We all lived in the same apartment complex,
back when I was just starting to speak Farsi
and Amir was still a baby.

But they left town, and we stayed,
and now the first thing they say when they come back
is, "Omid *jan*, you've gotten so big!"
or "*Joonam*, is that really Amir?!"

They kiss us too. A lot.
But it's not as creepy as it sounds, I promise.
Kissing family on the cheek is super normal for Iranians.
When you first see them, or when you're leaving them,
you show them love, with a kiss, or two, or three.

I lose track of how many kisses are proper
or the kiss count each person prefers,
so I stick to two kisses across the board
just to be safe.

It's nice, actually. It's the part of any *mehmooni*
that feels the fullest. Because it feels good
to know a person you barely see anymore
still loves you.

But when I think about my friends
at school, or the boys on the baseball team,
or the girls who pass notes in class,
my stomach turns,
thinking of what they might say
if they saw us all kissing.

So I always try
to do the kissing part
as quickly as I can.

Silk

Maman Joon and Dad are in the bedroom. She's showing him a small square rug. Silk. Because selling rugs is his vocation. His calling. He's not just some rug guy. He's one of the best. His new store is the biggest in the state. I listen through the crack in the door. The small silk rug is from Iran. From a city called Qom. Maman Joon wants to know if Dad has any rugs like it in the store. No. The size and the color make a piece like this quite rare. He has some that are similar but nothing quite like it. That's what she thought. It was given to her by her father, on her wedding day. Could he sell it? Dad is a little confused. Why? It's sentimental and unique! Well, we were thinking we could use a little extra money after moving to America. Don't be ridiculous, Dad insists. We can give you any money you need. No, Maman Joon *tarofs*, we don't need any. This is something we want to do. If you sell it, give us half the money, and keep half for you. My dad waits, then *tarofs* back: *"It is my honor to sell this rug for you. And when it sells, we will not take a cent."*

Tarof

Tarof is a Persian thing that's worth stopping to explain.

Tarof is saying no to things offered to you
even if you actually really want them.
Tarof is offering things to people
even if you don't actually want to give them.
Tarof is putting the concerns of others
before your own concerns.
Tarof is "We're not worthy" from *Wayne's World* —
times infinity.

Tarof is signing a long contract that you don't read.
Tarof is a performance and a prayer.
Tarof is manners on steroids.

Tarof is the Arnold Schwarzenegger of manners.

But *tarof*, as it assumes
and omits much, can also leave
really important things
unclear, uncertain,
or unspoken.

So, sometimes I think *tarof* is the Terminator of manners too.

Maybe *tarof* was sent here to destroy us.

Teaching Tarof

The last time I taught *tarof*
was a few years back, when Sammy
was sleeping over at my house.

He was confused when my mom
brought out some Oreos and milk after dinner,
after we already told her we weren't feeling dessert.

I guess Sammy was living in a world
where what he was feeling,
or what he wanted,
actually had some kind of impact
on parents' behavior.

"You don't have to eat them if you don't want.
It's a Persian thing."

I was already used to a world
of cookies when you weren't feeling cookies,
apologies when you weren't feeling sorry,
favors when you weren't feeling generous,
and service for the sake of tradition.

I thought it was nice of Mom, actually.
To bring out Oreos and milk,
instead of the usual tea and dates,
in an attempt to make Sammy feel comfortable.

We ended up taking the Oreos back to my room.

I ate them all.

Breakaway

We got up early today.
Before sunrise early.
To drive to my grandparents' house.
To watch soccer.
Iran is playing.
I'm wearing the T-shirt my uncle bought me in LA,
Karimi and Ali Daei on my chest, the Iranian flag on my back.
Maman Joon serves us *chai* with *noon o kareh o paneer.*
I'm spreading the butter and feta on my pita with my thumbs,
when suddenly Karimi breaks through the midfield,
flying past the defenders toward the goal,
and now Baba Joon and I are on our feet,
our hands clenched into fists
breath held, eyes wide,
as Karimi shoots
and the ball soars

                                                    crossbar
                                        the
                              over

The room erupts, then exhales.
We collapse into each other.
Snapping fingers, slapping backs,
we mourn the thing we almost had.
Then we settle in and wait
for another chance.

Baba Joon puts his arm around me . . .
and I suddenly feel so much
closer to him.

Not just because he's half hugging me,
but because we just went through something
pretty ordinary together, for the first time?
I've never watched soccer with my grandpa before.
There's so much we haven't done together, yet.

That's when he turns to me
and says in shaky English,
"It okay, Omid. We get another shot."

And I think
he's still talking about the game,
but maybe he's not.

Choose Right

All the incoming sophomores
sit in single-serving desks set up in lines
inside the gym to take our placement tests today.
The standardized kind, with No. 2 pencils to be sharpened,
bubbles to be filled, and answers to be scanned.
We take this test to be told
whether or not we are
gifted.

I don't think I am.
Gifted, that is.
I mean, I'm stumped
before the first question.

On the very first page,
they ask for your
Name
Birthday
and
Race.

American Indian or Alaska Native
Asian
Black or African American
White
Native Hawaiian or Pacific Islander

Confused
I raise my hand
and wait for Ms. Lowell
to see me.

"My parents are from Iran.
Iran is in Asia,
but I don't think
I'm the kind of Asian
they're asking about.

Which box do I check?"

She holds up a finger and nods,
returns to her desk, and takes out a big book,
probably the one with all the right answers in it,
then heads back toward me.

"White,"
she says quietly, as she returns.
"The proctor manual indicates all
students of Middle Eastern descent
should choose white."

"White?"

But I'm not white.
You don't have to be gifted
to see that.

Can I still choose it?

First Day Of School, 1990

"Maman, where are we?"

"Excuse me, we're looking for Mrs. Bowen's class . . ."
"It's all the way down the hall — first door on your right."

"Put me down! I want to walk!"

"Thank you so much.
Not yet, Omid, stop squirming, we're almost there."

Opening the door to Mrs. Bowen's pre-K classroom,
"It's okay, Omid jan. Everything is going to be okay . . ."
she said more to herself than to me.

I could feel my mom's heart beating fast in her chest
as she hugged me hard, then put me down on the floor.

"Hello, Mrs. Bowen, this is Omid.
He's very excited to start school today."
"Hello, Omid! It's nice to meet you.
I'm Mrs. Bowen. How are you doing?"

"Maman, who is this lady?"

"He doesn't speak English yet,
but he's very smart. He will learn fast."
"Of course, of course he will!
Hola, Omid. Me llamo Señora Bowen. ¿Cómo estás?"

"Maman, can we go home?"

"Oh no, not Spanish. Sorry. We are from Iran. He speaks Farsi."

"Oh no! I'm the one who should be sorry . . .
I don't know any . . . Farsi . . . to welcome you, Omid.
But I promise we're going to have a great time together.
Class? Can everyone say hello to your new classmate, Omid?"

"Omid jan, you are going to stay here today.
I will come back to get you soon.
Everything will be okay.
Make friends."

"No, Maman! I'm sorry!
I want to go home.
Please — don't go."

But she did.

She left because she thought it would be better for us both.
Then twenty-eight kids waved their hands in the air
and started to talk to me,
started to talk at me
in some language
I didn't understand.
I didn't know what to do.
I didn't know how to speak.
And for the first time I can remember,

I was scared.

Losing My Farsi

All I can tell you is that it happened slowly,
and it's hard to remember the specifics,
but I think it has to do with friendship.

Before I started going to school
everything was all smiles at home,
and my best friends were Mom and Dad,
and friends want friends to be comfortable,
and Mom and Dad were most comfortable
in Farsi.

After I started school, Mom and Dad realized
that to be the best mom and dad they could be,
they'd have to help me make new best friends,
closer to my age, like the kids at school,
who didn't speak any Farsi.

So they stopped speaking
so much Farsi at home.
They stopped just short
of making English
the official language
of our household.

I remember how
it sucked a whole lot at first,
until it sucked a little less
because Mom and Dad were right,
and eventually I started to learn
new words in a new language,

which helped me make new friends
who were all comfortable
in English.

But the smiles changed.

Especially the ones at home, which used to be full
of understanding, uninterrupted, and whole.
Over time, they creaked, they cracked,
they leaned,
uneven.

First Day Of School, 2001

School is a private affair.
Private in the literal sense.
I've been in college-prep school
since the sixth grade. A small class
is the only size class I've ever known.

But *this* class
                    is *smaller* than small.
This class
                    is *privater* than private.

Ten of us tested into
Ms. Lowell's sophomore Honors English class.
And if we do well this year, we can take AP English next year
and then go on to create our own independent studies as seniors.

Ten of us.

Andrea, Emily, Katie, Carlos, Rebecca,
Sarah, Melissa, Erik, David, and Omid.

Shy, but honored to be here,
eager to read and write,
and while we might
not admit it to each other,
for one reason or another,
we're all curious.
Ready to learn
what English
can really do
for us.

The First Book Of The Year

in Honors English . . . is a play?
Well played, Ms. Lowell!

A Midsummer Night's Dream
by William Shakespeare.

He's the real deal.
I read some of his plays in middle school,
and I just love the way he plays with words.
We don't know everything about him,
but what I remember learning in class
is seriously impressive.

Shakespeare grew up in a small town in England,
where we have no record of him ever finishing school.
Then he moved to London, where he started writing these
incredible poems and some of the greatest stories ever told,
where he became the queen's favorite playwright,
and even ended up partial owner of the Globe Theatre,
which is still the most famous theater in the world.

This small-town kid was on another level.

He had so many ideas — he had to make up new words
to express them all. Words we still use today, like
"bedroom," "bandit," "scuffle," and "unreal."
He turned nouns, like "elbow," into verbs.
He even invented the name "Jessica."
And yeah, I know it might sound nerdy,
but I think that's just . . . unreal.

How often does someone come around
who can change the way
we use a language?

For some reason, I remember
how proud my dad was,
when he said that thing
about the only real real
art being advertising.

And I laugh
as I imagine how Dad might
describe William Shakespeare.
He's the greatest writer of all time.
He's the greatest playwright of all time.

Baba, he's the greatest two-for-one deal of all time!

The New Kid Recap

Victoria Nova College Preparatory School
is a school in demand.

Meaning parents who care
about placement, and can afford to,
compete to send their kids our way.

Meaning each year
Nova High gets nova faces.
(New kids. Lots of them.)

Meaning most of our classes begin
with a recap of what we've already been taught,
just to make sure the whole class is on the same page.

Usually the teacher asks us some simple question
at the start of class, and the old Nova kids all stay silent
while the new Nova kids sweat it out a bit.

But Honors English was different.

The New Kid Recap was no match
for one of the new faces,
a girl named Emily Bishop.

Ms. Lowell asked us to define iambic pentameter.

Emily's hand flew up,
quickly at first,
then slowly as she realized
no one else was racing her to answer.

I thought that was pretty
funny, actually.

"Emily?"

"Yeah. Iambic pentameter is a line of verse or poetry
made up of five feet, one foot being an unstressed,
then stressed syllable.

It helps me when I think of language like music.

A line in pentameter
is like a measure in 5/4
with five quarter notes in it,
but each quarter note is split into eighth notes,
one unaccented, then one accented,
through the end of the measure."

"That's correct. And thank you for the wonderful analogy."

I had no idea what Emily was talking about.
But she did. And I liked that.
And, if I'm being honest,
she was kind of cute.
And I liked that too.

Trying To Escape My Body

After class I went to my locker
to swap out my English books for my math book,
when I saw that new girl, Emily,
walking across the courtyard
in my direction.

I wondered
if she'd noticed me in class
the way I'd noticed her.

But I hadn't spoken up, so,
I mean, why would she?
Of course she hadn't.

The closer she got,
the more my heart
started doing that thing
where it bangs up against my rib cage
like it's trying to escape my body.

I racked my brain
wondering what she could want with me.
As she knelt down to put her backpack on the ground,
time began to crawl. We were fully in slow motion now
as she reached up to touch . . .
the locker on my left.

She had the locker next to mine.
She was walking toward the locker.
Not toward me. Of course. Duh.
That makes perfect sense.

So why the hammering heart and the sudden sweating
on a surprisingly cool day in August, Omid?

Maybe it was her. Maybe it was how her dark hair
glowed golden brown when the sun hit it.
Or how her bright blue eyes peeked out
from behind her bangs. Or maybe
it was her freckles.

Let me make something clear:
I'm not the type to usually notice freckles.
Or bangs. Or hair glowing any color when the sun hits it.
And I'm especially not the type to want to start a conversation
with someone I don't really know. And sure, I guess I kinda
knew Emily a little from class just now, but then why
was my body so convincingly in stranger danger mode?

What would Sammy do?
He would say something.
And it would be totally natural.
But what would it be?

Emily was almost done doing whatever she was doing
and I actually wished I knew what she was doing
so I could maybe use that information to start a conversation
but if I looked over she might see me looking
and I wouldn't have anything to say yet
and she would think I was some kind of creep
and then she would ask for a new locker
so she didn't have to deal with the creep
who's always staring at her
with nothing to say.

She started walking away.

And all of a sudden I was exhausted.
Not sleepy. Just tired — of never having
words when I want them. When
I need to not be a nobody.

Is that a double negative? Or a triple negative?
Either way I'm always being negative . . .

I could try. To speak up.

To make it up to Mom and Dad
for forgetting Farsi and forever
cursing the family smile
in the name of friendship.
To make up for the *mehmoonis*,
where I rarely speak with
blood relatives and barely
bond with my grandparents.

At least Emily is new and doesn't know
I'm usually the quiet sidekick.

At least Emily and I can speak
the same language.

"Ohhh — hey!"

I said
out loud
quite loud.

49

Emily turned around. Looking a little scared
but mostly confused. Probably because
I was speaking at a much higher volume
than was necessary when in
such close proximity to
another human being.

I took a deep breath
and turned down my volume.

"So . . . have you read Shakespeare before?"

A Language Like Music

"Sorry, what?"

She was understandably confused.
I hadn't really started a conversation.
I'd fired a question into the air between us.

"Ummm . . . have you studied Shakespeare before?
It just sounded like you knew
what you were talking about back there."
"Ohhh, that. No, I never really studied him,
but I performed a scene from *Romeo and Juliet*
in drama class last year, and we had to learn
all about verse and meter. So, yeah . . ."

"That's awesome. I'm Omid, by the way."
"I'm Emily. I'm new here."
"Yeah, I was at Nova last year
and I don't remember you."
And then I laughed,
as if I had just said something funny.

"So . . . Have *you* read Shakespeare before, Omid?"
"Oh yeah, I read *Julius Caesar* a few years ago. It was gnarly."

Gnarly? *Julius Caesar* was gnarly?
Wow, Omid. Wow. Abort mission,
whatever this mission is . . .
Abort! Abort!

"But yeah . . . your explanation of iambic pentameter was
really specific. I'd never heard it described that way before."

"Oh, do you play music?"
Her eyes lit up.
Like, they actually got brighter. Like magic.
"No — um — I don't. Do you?"
"Yeah. My parents got me started on the piano
when I was younger. But I'm trying to learn guitar."
"Well, it sounds like you know — a lot — already.
About the quarters and dimes and measures at least.
I don't know much about that. Lots of people don't."

She laughed. A real laugh,
deeper than you'd expect. Not one of those
high-pitched laughs the girls let out in the cafeteria after
Jimmy Conley says literally anything.

It felt good. To make her laugh like that.
I didn't know what I'd done to earn it,
but I wanted to find out,
so I could do it again.

"Okay, so you're not a musician . . . but I bet you could still
figure it out. I mean, do you listen to music?"
"Totally." I lied. I didn't.
"Okay, great — who do you listen to?"
"Oh, lots of different people. But. Um —
I really like Tracy Chapman.
And Neil Diamond, too."
"Holy crap, dude. That's like what my parents listen to."

Of course it was.
Because it's what my parents listened to, too.
The truth is, I never really "got into" music.
Like, I'll listen to whatever is on in the background, I guess,

but if I have free time, I'm not just going to listen to music
randomly. I'd rather be reading or playing video games.
Except for when I'm in the car with my parents.
And we roll down the windows
and we turn up the volume
and we sing along.
But I'll be honest,
most of the time
the music blasting
out of our car
is very, very
Persian.

And I didn't think Emily would be familiar with Googoosh,
or Dariush, or Black Cats, or Sandy, or Andy.
So I went with the two American musicians
I'd heard enough of in the car to know their names.
Tracy Chapman (Mom's car) and Neil Diamond (Dad's car).

"Maybe our first step should be getting you
to listen to some better music . . ."
Our first step? Our?
"I'm down. I mean, I'm always looking out for new stuff."
"Are you?"
I nodded confidently.
As if I was a person who was actually
always looking out for *new stuff*.
"Okay then. I'll burn you a CD. Cool?"
"Cool."

Cool.

We Will Never Know

My dad gets home from work
and asks me to walk on his back.

I've been doing this for years
but we both know
I'm getting too big
too heavy
too grown
to keep doing it
much longer.

I take off my shoes and my socks
as Dad turns on the TV and tunes in
to *20/20*, *60 Minutes*, or CNN.

Dad watches the news
every single night.

He takes off his shirt
and lies facedown on the floor,
turning his head toward the TV.

He inhales.
I put one foot on his back,
my skin touching his,
searching for the strongest
part of him.

He nods his head
to tell me I've found it.

He exhales.
I step up, finding my balance
on the man who made me,
somewhere between his ribs.
I feel him give over to my weight,
my pressure relieving his.

I am afraid
that I will break him,
that I might take a wrong step and hurt him so bad
that he'll never be able to walk again.

He's come so far
from where he started —
why do I feel like I'll be the reason
he can't keep going?

There's a breaking
news report: a black man
has been killed
by a gun
by a policeman
by a thing that is good
at killing.

Dad nods at me again, this time signaling
the massage is over. I step off his back
and he puts on his shirt. Then he turns to me
and says, "What they do to them in this country,
how they treat them,
we will never know
how that feels."

Another Sunday, Another Mehmooni

"Omid tested into Honors English at school!"
Mom says, as she serves her mother's *sabzi polo ba mahi sefeed*
onto Baba Joon's plate.

"Congratulations, Omid! My grandson's English is excellent!
Maybe he will use his excellent English and the notebook I
brought him from Tehran to write poetry, to be the next
great Persian poet! Are we all sharing a meal
with the next Hafez? Or the next Rumi?"
Baba Joon says, looking toward me,
smiling, raising his bushy eyebrows.

"I've already started writing in it! It's my journal now,"
I say out loud, at first excited and to Baba Joon,
and then embarrassed and to no one in particular
because I forgot that I wasn't speaking Farsi.

"He says he's already writing in it, Baba.
It's his diary," Mom chimes in.

"Wonderful! Of course he is."

I don't know what to say,
or how I would say it if I did.
I could try. To speak, to correct
my mom, to find the word
for "journal" in Farsi
(which is what I said)
and to not settle for "diary"
(which is what she said for me).
I could try.

But.
What if the words
don't show up? Or worse.
What if I mistake one word for another
and say the wrong thing?

Like last year, when I asked Dad
to pass the "*shotor zard*" after dinner
and he started laughing so hard he almost spit out his tea.
"*Sholeh zard, Omid jan*," my mom corrected me.

I meant to ask him to pass the "rice pudding,"
but apparently I asked him to pass the "yellow camel."

What would Baba Joon think
if he saw me make a mistake like that?
That I'm thick. In more ways than one.
So I just look down at my plate.

Sabzi polo ba mahi sefeed translates to
"green rice with white fish,"
and as far as Persian food goes, it's simple.
It's one of the very few times
where the name of the dish
is pretty much also the entire recipe.
But with Iranians, even what appears simple
usually isn't.

The rice is green because it's cooked
with a mixture of chopped herbs,
and good luck finding a mom who will just tell you
their unique amalgamation.

The fish is a white fish, sure, but not just any cod or tilapia
(though those might do in a pinch).
For the real dish you need the real fish,
and for the real fish you need a special talk
with the grocer at the special shop
that only Middle Easterners know exists,
a fragrant hole in the wall
in downtown Tucson.

Mom's *sabzi polo* is pretty great.
But Maman Joon's is even better.

She must be using a different mixture.

We usually eat this dish in March.
March 21st, to be exact.
On *Nowruz* (the Persian New Year).
Because it's a dish you eat to celebrate.

Tonight we're "celebrating" my Honors English placement, sure,
but that's just one side of the story. There's also something else
we're gathered to celebrate. Something more important.
The memory of a person I never met.
Tonight we're celebrating
a whole life.

Longingly, Long Enough

After dinner, Maman Joon serves tea
like she always does, dark and hot.

I don't usually drink it. I don't really like the taste.
But sometimes tea means more than tea,
and this is clearly one of those times.

So I sit on the floor in their living room, sip the bitter liquid,
and suck on *ghand* (a sugar cube) to make it go down easy,
as my family circles up on sofas and spare chairs,
like a group of kids playing ring-around-the-rosy
ashes ashes we all fall down
to remember a person
who should have
been there
with us.

There is a framed photo of Baba Joon's sister on the table.
Baba Joon looks at it longingly, long enough
for the room to notice, to quiet, and then
he tells us about her.

She was born fifty-four years ago today.
She was martyred exactly thirty-five years later.

She was a hard worker, earnest and honest.
She believed in people. In something bigger than herself.

She gave more than she had to give.
She hoped others would do the same.

She liked to read, but often fell asleep mid-page.
She liked the beach, but never got in the water.

She had an answer for everything.
She knew how to laugh well.

He tells us her name was Azadeh,
and tonight we are gathered to remember her,
to celebrate her, to love her, and to miss her.

Baba Joon is quiet again.
He looks around the room
at each of us. His eyes land on me last.
I am quiet too. I'm thinking about the word
azadeh and how I'm pretty sure it means "freedom" in Farsi.
I'm thinking how hard a name it must have been
to live up to during a revolution.
I'm thinking about how she died.
Hung, in public. I'm wondering —
is she free now?

Baba Joon tilts his head, like he knows what I'm thinking,
like he's about to say something.
But instead, he just smiles
and closes his eyes.

And then

Baba Joon begins to sing.

When Baba Joon Sings

he cries
for his sister who was killed
in Iran for praying.

When Baba Joon sings

he prays
and I start to believe
prayer is powerful.

When Baba Joon sings

I don't understand
what he's saying,
but I know exactly
what he means.

The Farsi he sings is unlike any Farsi I've ever heard.
The sentences are longer and the expressions more foreign.
The whole language has grown ancient,
right before my very ears.

But there's something timeless in it, too.
There's music in it.

The words move
in a rhythm
that moves me.

The tone of his voice
soars and dives,

beyond meaning,
beyond mourning,
becoming something
almost joyful.

It pushes me past
knowing, toward some
kind of understanding.

It makes me feel
instead of think.

It makes me wonder,

how in the world
did Baba Joon
just do that?

Between Here And Home

It's late.

Dad drives us home
in his new Mercedes SL.
Amir and I are crammed into a back row
that was not designed with family in mind,
somewhere between awake and asleep and pain and comfort,
eyelids getting heavy, every blink getting longer.

Mom is in the passenger seat.
She's telling Dad a story about Azadeh,
who always went on walks and brought home
the brightest flowers.

Mom still dreams about those flowers.
Sometimes she can still smell them as she wakes up.
Dad reaches over and squeezes her hand.
Tears roll down her cheeks.

Strange, I think.

Mom's voice is so steady,
I would have never known she was crying
if I hadn't opened my eyes.

September 11th, 2001

My mom and I
thought it was a prank
or a bad joke on the radio
about all the airports in America
being shut down.

She dropped me off at school
and kissed me goodbye,
but it wasn't a prank.

Two buildings in New York
were hit by planes.
People were trapped
above the flames
and decided to jump.
For some reason,
I thought of an old myth,
of Icarus, of the wax
melting
off his wings
when he flew
too close to the sun.

Then both buildings collapsed.

And everyone died.
Even the people
who held out hope,
who never jumped.

We watched it happen

live on the TVs
meant for special occasions
in our classrooms
meant for studying world events.
It didn't feel real
until our teachers started crying.
An announcement was made:
it was okay
for our parents
to come pick us up.

On the way home,
Mom is dazed.

Her mouth isn't moving
but her face says it all.

Her face
looks like mine
sometimes.

Like she's trying to find
the right words
in the right order.

And I want to tell her
it's okay. I know
how that feels.

Like she's trying to keep me
from worrying.

And I want to tell her

it's okay. I'm not
worried.

I want to tell her the truth.

The truth is
I feel lucky.

Lucky we don't live in New York,
or some other big city
that these evil people
might want
to attack.

The truth is
I feel lucky.

I don't know anyone who died today,
and I get to spend a day at home,
and tomorrow
everything will go back
to normal.

The Sign

Dad got home later than usual.
I was lying on the couch asleep
and then pretending
to be asleep.
Dad kissed Mom on the cheek.
She kissed him back.

Silence.

Dad spoke first, in Farsi.
"Are you okay?"

"I can't believe it. I can't believe it. But, yes. I'm okay. You?"

"I'm fine. Everything will be alright, dear."

*"But what will people do?
Should I keep Omid and Amir at home tomorrow?"*

*"No, we should send them to school.
We shouldn't do anything out of the ordinary.
We don't want to scare the boys."*

*"But — shouldn't they be scared?
Don't you remember — 1979, the revolution —
how it was for us here after they took the hostages in Tehran?"*

*"This time it has nothing to do with Iran.
The Arabs are taking credit. Besides, we've been here
for over twenty years. My phone was ringing all day.
Our friends are asking if we want to stay with them*

in their homes. People have changed.
They know us."

"But why are they offering their homes then?
Because they know what might happen — to our home.
They know what the idiots and ignorant strangers might do."

"Don't be ridiculous. Everyone knows us here.
Nothing bad is going to happen."

Dad said it as if
he was trying
to convince
himself more
than Mom.

"I saw a man this morning
standing at the intersection after I dropped Omid off.
As soon as the planes hit. He wasn't asking for money.
He was holding a sign above his head.

A few hours later, on the way to pick up the kids, I saw him again.
He was still there, Reza. I had to take another street home
so Amir and Omid wouldn't see."

"Why? What did the sign say?"

And this part
this part
Mom said
in English.

"Nuke Iran."

The Most Muslim Thing About My Dad

He won't eat bacon.
Not with breakfast, not ever.
I tell him, over and over,
how delicious it is. Not to torture him,
but because I want him to try it.
I want him to taste what I taste.
I want him to feel what I feel.
I want him to enjoy
what I enjoy.

But he doesn't.

Instead, he just smiles and says,
"This way there's more for you, *baba*."

The Most Muslim Thing About Me

is my dad. Which is no small thing. Even though
I'm not Muslim and don't think I ever will be.

Sometimes it helps me to think of life like math.

Or more specifically, algebra.

(Which was invented by a Persian
Muslim dude like my dad, by the way.)

So let's say two people are represented by two variables
in an equation. In this case, x is Reza (my dad)
and y is Shohreh (my mom).

One day these variables meet, and they like each other,
and they multiply . . . creating xy (or me).

IF
the x is Muslim
and the y is Bahá'í

THEN
that makes me both.

Even if I don't believe in any of it.

It's still a part of me.

The New Me

As we sat in the same seats
we sat in to watch the towers fall
just a few days ago,
Ms. Lowell tried
to carry on with the lessons
she had planned.

Nothing had really changed inside our classroom,
but it felt like the world was starting to change outside of it.
Like everyone thought we knew what we could expect
out there, but it turns out we were all wrong,
and people died because of it.
And we didn't want to look at it.
Not too closely.
Not yet.

Instead, we turned back to books.
Back to Billy Shakespeare.

Ms. Lowell was joined by Mr. Thompson in class today
to announce a collaboration between the English department
and the theater department.

A Midsummer Night's Dream
will be the fall/winter show at Nova High.
First we're going to read the play
and discuss its "literary merits" in English class.
Then the ten of us will be "encouraged,
even offered extra credit, to audition
for the school's production."

I noticed my eyes wandering in Emily's direction,
maybe because she'd told me about performing Shakespeare
at her last school, or maybe my eyes have just been looking
for any excuse to find Emily
as often as they can.

She saw me see her, and she smiled.

Then she looked around the room
to see if anyone else was looking
at her — or looking at me looking at her?
I don't know.

But what I did know
was that Emily had done *Romeo and Juliet* last year,
which means she might do *Midsummer* this year.

Extra credit doesn't mean much to me.
I don't need the extra work,
because my grades are already great.
But this . . . this could be even better
than getting great grades.

This could mean extra time with Emily,
which is the opposite of extra work.
This could mean even more than that.
Being in this play could even be the way
to get people to finally see me differently.
This could be what I've been waiting for.

This could be the thing that changes everything.
This could be the new me.

Proposal

I packed up my backpack,
planned my proposal,
then made my way to
her desk by the door.

I'd never really done this before.

"Hey, Emily . . ."
"Hey, Omid!"

Her fingernails were painted blue
and somehow seemed to have the power
to remove any and all previous plans
from my brain.

"Hey — so —
I was just wondering
if you'd wanna, maybe,
audition for the play?"

She nodded but didn't respond,
as if she knew I'd forgotten to ask
the most important part
of that question.

"Oh,
          I mean,   like,
audition,
          with me,
for it,
                    together."

Each word fell out of my mouth,
plummeting toward the ground,
desperate to burrow into the cool comfort
of the earth's crust, eager to erase itself
from existence.

But she caught them all
before they could
disappear.

"Of course," she said.
"I'd totally love that.
I was hoping someone
would ask me."

I Don't Know What I Expected

but it definitely wasn't this.
It wasn't her saying yes!!!

Taking A Hike

Euphoria is short-lived, it seems.

When we got home from school, Mom told us
that Baba Joon wants to take Amir and me
on a hike this Sunday.

Which is not only a bit of a bummer, but also weird,
cuz that's when we usually have our *mehmoonis*.
And I guess I was actually expecting one, expecting us
to get together, especially after this week,
after what happened in New York.
I was expecting us all
to talk about it.

But instead, Baba Joon wants to hike.
So — we're going to go on a hike.

Amir is excited.
I am not.

I wish we were doing literally anything else.
I've never liked hiking.
Or more honestly,
I've never understood the point.
Our ancestors spent thousands of years
developing science and technology,
they built fires, then walls, then wheels, then air conditioners,
only for us to abandon it all? For fun?!
Disrespectful, if you ask me.
But Mom says I should go.

"Baba Joon is very excited. He loves to hike,
and he wants to spend quality time with his grandsons.
Don't worry, Omid, you'll be fine.
He used to take me with him all the time
when I was younger."

I think about Baba Joon
raising the little-girl version of my mom in Iran,
how they loved going to the movies, or seeing plays,
or going shopping, or trying out new restaurants,
or going on hikes.

Then I think about Baba Joon
going to the grocery store last week
and not knowing how to tell
the difference between the packages
of sour cream, cottage cheese, and margarine.
So he bought them all, just to be safe,
and brought them home,
thinking one of them had to be
yogurt.

I realize
how many simple things
are now difficult.

I realize
taking a hike is the same
wherever you are.

"Okay, Mom, I'll go."

Go Back

I'm reading a book in my bedroom
and just learned the past tense of "hang,"
like when you hang someone, is "hanged."
I'm pretty sure I wrote "hung" earlier.

I wish I could go back
and fix it.

It's Early

Too early to be awake on a Sunday.
The sun isn't even up.
But I am.

I guess this is when people
go on hikes.

An Adventure

I've been to Sabino Canyon before,
with Mom and her friends, or Dad and Amir.
We've walked up the mountain,
on the paved path, crossing over
cobblestone bridges, jumping over
tiny streams, four miles up,
four miles down.

It takes hours. It's always hot. It's never fun.
I still don't know how anyone
could get excited about it.

But to my surprise,
Baba Joon doesn't look too excited either.
Maybe Sabino is not the kind of canyon he expected.

He came prepared with a fanny pack,
water bottles, and even a wooden cane.
But when he sees the paved path,
filled with amateur hikers of all ages,
he changes his mind about something.

He walks us up the path,
determined to show us how
to pass as many slow walkers as possible.
And when we've trekked far enough,
when the parking lot and pedestrians
are finally out of view, he stops,
turns to Amir and me, and says,

"Let's go on an adventure."

Big Cats

Baba Joon wants to take us off the paved path
and into the desert,
as in the wilderness,
as in with the wildlife,
as in I think this is a bad idea.

Amir takes off,
already leading the way,
probably getting too close to all the cacti,
and Baba Joon is running behind him,
happy in a way I haven't seen him happy before.
But I'm still standing on the pavement.
I'm thinking of all those animals and insects
that are most definitely out there
just waiting to bite me.

Baba Joon turns around and sees me stalled.
"What happened, Omid? What's wrong?"

I don't have the stomach for this.
But more importantly,
I don't have the words for this.

I'm always like this.
            Frozen in Farsi but desperate to thaw.
                    I've been through one too many *mehmoonis*
                of not speaking up for myself.
                Of settling for someone else's translation.
        But no one's here now — except me and him.
And the last time I didn't know how to speak,
to Emily at school, I just —

did it anyway. And now she's making me a mix CD.
          And sure — I don't expect Baba Joon to make me a mix —
    but maybe I could just try
                    to speak anyway.

I don't know how to say,
"I'm afraid of yellow-jacket wasps."
So instead, I say,
"Flies."

Baba Joon smiles.
He reaches into his bright blue fanny pack
and takes out a can of bug spray.
"For flies."

I don't know how to say,
"What if we run into a mountain lion?"
So instead, I say,
"Big cats."

Baba Joon runs back toward me.
He calls out to Amir and tells him to join us.

*"Boys, when we go into the desert,
we have to stay together.
As long as you're both near me,
you have nothing to be afraid of.
As long as I am here,
I will protect you."*

Amir doesn't really ever need protection,
so understandably he is unconcerned.
But I'm evaluating the risk here.

Baba Joon might mean well,
but he's just an old man
with a little cane
in a big desert.

My face betrays my thoughts.
He's been watching me the whole time.
He's seen my eyes darting back and forth,
between his face and his cane.
I'm embarrassed.

But Baba Joon smiles.

He puts down his water bottle
and lifts his cane up to his chest.
He grabs the handle with one hand.
He grabs the bottom with his other hand.
He pulls hard and twists
until the cane splits
into two.

In one hand, Baba Joon is holding a hollow wooden staff.
In the other hand, Baba Joon is holding the handle,
now attached to
a long silver
blade.

Baba Joon's cane just turned into a sword.
Still smiling, he looks at me and says,

"For big cats."

The Most Important Job

"Amir, you lead the way.
You are free to take us
wherever you want to go,
but not too far too fast.
To be a good leader, you must
worry about the well-being
of those who follow you.

Omid, you, on the other hand, must worry less."

This is something people say to me
from time to time, and I always clock it.
They say it like they're members of some club
that's always comfortable. A club
I never got invited to join
but they all expect me
to be a part of.

"Omid, are you listening? Worry less, joonam.
Instead, I want you focused on your job . . .
You have the most important job."
Baba Joon opens his fanny pack and pulls out
a ziplock bag full of small green toothpick flags.
"I want you to take these flags and place them
in the ground every few meters, as we go."

Once again, Amir gets to captain and command.
He gets to set the course, and I get a bag of toothpicks.
There's a metaphor for you.

"Baba Joon . . . do I have to?"

"Of course! Of course you have to, Omid.
How will we ever find our way home
if there is nothing to remind us
where we came from?"

Running Toward The Water

I underestimated how far we could walk.

It's been hours.
It's been weeks.
It's been years
of looking out for rattlesnakes.
It's gotten significantly hotter.
My feet hurt, my legs hurt,
and I'm getting dangerously close
to failing my one and only job.

I overestimated how many flags were in the bag.

I start thinking about rationing the remaining flags,
or asking Baba Joon if we can just turn around,
when I hear the sound
of rushing water.

We turn a corner. I can't believe what I'm seeing.
Amir somehow led us to a waterfall
right in the middle
of the desert.

"Amir, did you know this was here?!"

But he can't hear me.
He's already running full speed ahead
toward the water. And Baba Joon can't hear me
because he's running too.

To Swim Or Not To Swim

"Jump in, Omid, come join us!"
"No, I'm good."

Baba Joon gets out of the water and walks over to me.
"Omid, are you really? Good?"
"I'm fine."
"So why not swim?"

I can't keep this up. Not in Farsi.
I know Baba Joon understands a bit of English.
Not as much as I understand Farsi. But enough.
So I make the switch.

"I'm not the kind of person who jumps in the water.
Amir is the kind of person who jumps in the water."

"Who says?"

Who says? I don't know who says.
All I know is that it's true.

*"Listen to me. This desert does not know who you are.
It has no expectations of you.
It cannot judge you.
It can only be
by your side.*

Do you know why I love to hike, Omid?"

I shake my head: no.

"Because there are no people,
no strangers, no systems out here.
And where there are no people,
there are no roles to play,
no rules to define you.
In nature you can be
whoever you want to be."

The new me.

I walk toward the water.
I'm still scared to jump.
I slip off my shoes
and slowly
step in.

The water is cold.
But the longer I stay in it,
the more comfortable it gets.
I swim out farther. I even
take off my shirt.

Amir swims over to me
with a big idea brewing:

"Soooo — should we teach Baba Joon
how to play Marco Polo?"

We do.

And we play all day.

A Scene From Honors English

MS. LOWELL
Many of Shakespeare's best plays examine our expectations.

Ms. Lowell stands in front of her whiteboard,
leading the class in a discussion.

MS. LOWELL
What do we expect from the world, and what do we expect from
each other? In his play *As You Like It*, he even proposes: "All the
world's a stage, / And all the men and women merely players."
He does this in *Midsummer*, too, in a way. He asks us to think
about what we expect — of our surroundings, and of each other.
For example: Who can tell me why the mechanicals rehearse their
play in the forest?

DAVID
The mechanicals?

MELISSA
Snug, Quince, Flute, Starveling, Snout, and Bottom.

DAVID
Oh, the actors . . .

MS. LOWELL
That's right, the theater troupe. Puck calls them mechanicals
because they're craftsmen and laborers, not professional actors.
So, who knows why they are rehearsing in the woods?

ANDREA
They probably don't have a house big enough to fit them all in

Athens. I mean, they're laborers, not royals.

MS. LOWELL
A good point, Andrea. And practically speaking, that could
be true, but maybe there's another, more thematic, reason
Shakespeare chose that setting?

ERIK
The forest is where the fairies live!

The students all laugh.

MS. LOWELL
As funny as it may sound to some of you, Erik is onto something
here! But remember, the mechanicals didn't know about the
fairies when they decided to rehearse there . . .

OMID
They rehearse in the forest because . . .
in nature you can be
whoever you want to be.

MS. LOWELL
That's right, Omid! That is exactly right.

Emily's CD

After class, Emily gives me a CD,
each song a song she chose
just for me.

The King of Carrot Flowers, Pt. 1 — Neutral Milk Hotel
The Calendar Hung Itself . . . — Bright Eyes
Screaming Infidelities — Dashboard Confessional
The Middle — Jimmy Eat World
Undone (The Sweater Song) — Weezer
Sweetness — Jimmy Eat World
All the Small Things — blink-182
Adam's Song — blink-182
Photograph — Weezer
Wish You Were Here — Incubus
The Awful Sweetness of Escaping Sweat — Bright Eyes
We're at the Top of the World — The Juliana Theory
Sunrise, Sunset — Bright Eyes
Drive — Incubus
Minority — Green Day
Brain Stew — Green Day
I Felt Your Shape — The Microphones

Some Battle In Some War

I'm trying to finish my homework.
Upstairs. I'm reading about soldiers
in some battle in some war,
but I'm distracted. Frustrated. Annoyed.
Downstairs. Mom is playing music
loud. And she's singing along
in Farsi — and that's loud too.

I head down to ask her to stop,
or at least turn it down,
while I'm trying to read.

The house smells like a garden

of Eden, sweet herbs
simmering over a low heat
with turmeric, onions, and oil.
That can only mean one thing:
she's making *ghormeh sabzi.*

I see Mom dancing as she sets our *sofreh,*
a traditional — beautiful —
piece of fabric Persians put food on.
It billows in the air
before falling to the floor.
She flattens out the wrinkles
and starts to set tiny bowls
filled with pickles and *torshi*
at each person's place.

(*Torshi* is delicious.
It's basically pickles
made of anything
but cucumbers.)

Mom is making a dinner
she's seen her mother make
a thousand times before
but over the years has
made her own.

Mom is happy.

Maman Joon is coming over tonight,
and Mom gets to share
her new version
of an old family
recipe.

I feel my frustration float away.
And now, I don't want anything to change.
But she turns around and sees me
and lowers the volume anyway.
"Yes, *joonam? Sorry, I didn't see you!*"

I don't want to tell her I was annoyed.
I don't want this moment to spoil.
I need something else to say . . .

"It's all good, Mom.
No — I just came down to ask —

ummm — how do you say
'yellow-jacket wasp' in Farsi?"

"What?"
"'Yellow-jacket wasp' in Farsi. How would I say that?"
"I don't know if we have that in Iran."

Interesting. That's good to know. That makes me feel
a little less shitty about my hiccup on the hike.
Or wait . . . does my mom just not know
what a yellow-jacket wasp is?

"But you could say *zamboor*, which means 'bee.'"
So she does know. Good.
"*Zamboor*. Right. Duh."
"Why do you ask, baby?"

Mom does this sometimes. Calls me "baby."
She's been doing it my whole life.
It's embarrassing when there are other people around,
but when it's just the two of us . . .
I don't mind it so much.

"Oh, no reason. I was just wondering.
Thanks, Mom."

Back Upstairs

I decide I'm done with homework.

Mom's music is back on full blast,
which reminds me,
I've got music
of my own now too.

I take Emily's CD out of my backpack,
load it up into my Walkman,
put on headphones,
and press play.

Heart Beats

So there's this song on Emily's CD that I really like.
Track 4. I know I like it a lot, because my index finger knows
exactly how many skips or rewinds it takes to get
to that track from anywhere else on the CD,
even when I'm not looking at my Walkman.

Listening to this song
feels like letting something go, something glide,
pressure releasing you didn't know was building up inside,
getting softer, getting stronger at the very same time.
It feels like falling down, but not wiping out,
just stumbling and getting right back up again.
Like falling was a part of the plan.

The song is called "The Middle"
by a band called Jimmy Eat World.
And when the chorus takes off,
the band rises to the occasion,
and the lead singer locks in, singing
over and over that everything
will be just fine, insisting
that everything
will be alright.

And every time I hear it, that kick drum
beating beneath the bass line like a heart,
like my heart beats around Emily,
I want to believe
everything
could be
alright.

Beneath The Mesquite

She left it there. On my hand!
The bottom of HER hand on
the top of MY hand, soft!

Wait, wait, I'm getting ahead of myself.
Let me set the scene . . .

It was lunch, and Emily asked me
if I wanted to rehearse our audition for *Midsummer*.
She'd picked a scene and thought we should give it a read.
I said "Of course," and we sat outside the cafeteria,
at the blue metal picnic table
beneath the mesquite tree.
"You be Lysander," she said,
"and I'll be Hermia."
We read the scene, sitting side by side.
It was hot outside. But this felt nice.
We said the words, kind of half
acting the parts, torso-acting
in the breeze, with our lower bodies
glued to the hot blue bench,
half Lysander and Hermia,
half Omid and Emily,
and that's when

she put her hand on mine.

I couldn't remember my next line.

                              I didn't want to
                        remember my next line.

Just then, Sarah ran over
and asked Emily if she could copy her homework.
But Emily just left her hand on mine.
She definitely put her hand there as Hermia,
but I think she left it there as Emily.

Emily got rid of Sarah. I still didn't know what
to do, and now I was starting to worry
that it was getting awkward.

I didn't know if I was touching Hermia or Emily anymore.

I needed something, anything, to do, to say . . .
and that's when I remembered: there was a script!
A literal literary genius had already figured it out for me!
I just needed to reach for the script . . .

I pulled my hand away —

> No! Stupid! So stupid!
> Why did I do that??

"Sorry about Sarah. We swap homework at lunch every day,
but I forgot to find her. Ummm . . . okay, let's try this again?
From the top of the scene?"

> Again! Yes! Of course!
> Let's do that again.

But as we reached the same part of the scene
I put out my hand, and this time,
Hermia's hand didn't meet it.
This time, Omid's hand just sat
on the picnic table all alone,
while Emily pretended
not to notice.

A First

I'm at home
hanging out on the sofa
reading through *Midsummer*
when the phone rings.

Mom picks up.
I hear her ask who it is.
"Amir is at soccer practice now,
but I'll tell him you called."
Silence.

"Oh — Omid?"

She shoots me a look that somehow says,
"Job well done" and "That's a first"
at the same time. I start to wonder
who could be on the line . . .

"Yes, he's here! Hold one moment."
She switches to Farsi. *"Well, well, well!
Omid, my handsome boy, there's a young lady
on the phone for you! She sounds very pretty.
Her name is — Emily?"*

My stomach drops
through the sofa, through the floor,
through the earth's molten core,
and silently explodes into deep space
somewhere on the other side of the planet.

For the love of all things, I pray Emily did not understand

a single word or even an intonation
of what my mom just said.

"GIVE ME THE PHONE RIGHT NOW,"
I whisper-scream.

Then I run over to take the phone/situation out of her hands
and sprint up the stairs to my room
as my mom whisper-laughs her heart out.

"Uh — hello?"
"Hi, Omid! It's Emily. From school."
"Hey, Emily! What's — um — up?"
"I looked your number up in the school directory.
I hope you don't mind."

Mind? Me? Nope. Not at all.
I absolutely do not mind any of this.
"No worries. Sorry, one sec,
I'm just walking up to my room."
I close my door.
I lock my door.
I look at my door.
I catch my breath.
Is this really happening?
I sit on my bed and say,
"I'm — glad you called."

"Oh, good! I was hoping you wouldn't think it was weird . . .
I just wanted to ask you how you thought today went?"

Good

How I thought today went . . .

Is she talking about our scene?
Or is she talking about our hand incident?
I should proceed with caution.
I should proceed with confidence.

But most importantly —
I should proceed.

"Good." I manage a single-word response.

"Yeah? Same! I think the scene gives us a lot to play with.
Like they're both so upset about their given circumstances,
but they are desperate to retain their agency.
They still try to do something about it, ya know?
They won't just sit there and let the world happen to them."

Okay, so Emily definitely undersold
how into this acting thing she is. She knows so much,
about drama, and about music.
What doesn't this girl do?
I have to keep up.

"Yeah, totally. I mean — that must be really frustrating.
Could you even imagine?"
"Honestly . . . kind of.
My dad moves around a lot for his job.
He says he put his foot down this time
and that we're going to be staying in Tucson for a while.
But he's said that all before. And yeah —

I just know how it feels when the world is making
these huge decisions for you."

Hold the phone . . .
She's not only new to Nova,
she's new to Tucson too?
Her dad moves around
a lot for his job?
Does that mean
she might leave?
That I could lose her
as quickly as I met her?

That hurts. And it hasn't even happened yet.

"Oh man, Emily. That really sucks."

And then I have an idea. Because I have to know . . .

"It must make things really hard for you
and your friends and your boyfriend
to be split up like that."

"Yeah, well, I don't have many of those to worry about . . .
But I figure it'll be worth it someday.
It's like you say in our scene,
'The course of true love
never did run smooth.'
I believe that. I do.
And that's why I really like Shakespeare.
He takes a lot of what's ugly out there
and makes it beautiful."

"I really like that too."

It's true. I loved doing the scene today.
I loved being with Emily.
But I loved the language too.
The sound of the words out loud.
I'm about to tell her my favorite line
about Hermia's rosy cheeks being pale
and how Shakespeare compares them
to actual roses needing water,
when Emily says,

"Well, hey, I gotta get going,
cuz my mom needs the phone.
But I'm excited to audition on Friday.
It's going to be a lot of fun.
I think we're good together."

And then I probably said something
like yeah okay see ya later I'm excited too
the scene is great for sure it's gonna be so fun,
but honestly, I can't remember what I said
or even what language I was speaking,
because Emily Bishop is amazing
and Emily Bishop had just said
that we were good
together.

And Then It Was Friday

and the audition went great. SO GREAT.

Seriously, it was more fun than I ever expected.

First, Emily and I did our scene:
Lysander and Hermia making plans
to run away and finally be
together

and it was perfect.

It went like we'd rehearsed. Maybe even better.
I barely had to look at the words,
because I almost knew them all
by heart.

We ended up holding hands at that one part
and even got a little bit of applause
from the small crowd watching
while they waited
to audition.

Mr. Thompson liked it too.

He said he didn't need to see any more
from the two of us because "That was just wonderful!"
Emily gave me a huge hug and it felt — whoa.
Like ohhhhh, this is what that heaven thing feels like,
wonderful, and warm, and everything right.

But then, as we were grabbing our backpacks to leave,

Mr. Thompson walked up to me and asked
if I wanted to stick around
to try some other sides
by myself.

> "Sides" are what he called the pieces of script
> he picked to audition the actors for parts —
> and he wasn't asking everybody
> to do more of them.

> I had a pretty good feeling going.
> And I wasn't ready to let that feeling end.
> So I said yes.

I hoped Emily might wanna hang out and watch,
but she took off as Mr. Thompson gave me the new sides
for a character named Bottom.

Bottom was a mechanical, one of the craftsmen
trying to be an actor. I remembered him from class.
But with a new script in hand,
and Emily nowhere to be seen,
I realized I might be
in over my head.

I'd start reading a line onstage
but would have to stop and look down at the sides
because I didn't understand . . .
I finally had to ask.

"Sorry, Mr. Thompson, I don't know if I follow.
Does he really mean to say '*monstrous* little voice'?
Or 'rehearse most *obscenely*'?"

Bottom kept saying the wrong thing
at the wrong time, moving through each line
like it didn't even matter.

"Yes! Good catch, Omid.
Bottom is not a Lysander type.
You can shake that all off now . . .

Bottom is a weaver.
Just a working-class guy, not fancy
like Lysander. Bottom is big and boisterous
and a bit of a buffoon. You should feel free to lean into it."

Lean *into* saying the *wrong* thing?

What an idea. What an escape
from the overwhelming weight
of trying to find
the right thing
to say.

Being Bottom

It didn't make much sense, at first,
but Shakespeare knew a thing or two,
and he wrote it, so maybe,
just maybe, there was
something to it.

I took a moment to really read the lines.
Then I went back onstage
and gave it a try.

I leaned into all of Bottom's wrong words
to see if they would push back
or catch me.

And something just — clicked.

Like a puzzle piece
sliding satisfyingly
into its perfect place.

Like I'd somehow
been preparing for this
my whole life.

When I was all done,
Mr. Thompson started clapping from the audience.
I could tell he was happy. I was happy too.

When I was playing Bottom, I felt like me. But different.
Even *more* me. Like bigger. But not bad bigger. *Brave* bigger.
And I never knew that was possible.

To be braver and bigger
and somehow   ~ *lighter* ~
at the same time.

To be weightless.

To be Bottom is to be bottomless.
Bottom just keeps going, growing more confident,
past protests and jests from his friends. He never gets
embarrassed — he only gets louder. And the louder he gets,
the lighter I get, until I'm floating, and

I don't ever have to come back down to earth.

In Between

After the audition,
that feeling lingers
as I float over to the baseball field,
as I wait for Sammy
to get out of practice.
He sees me and walks over.
"Yo. How was the audition thing?"
"It was — great."

Sammy nods, expecting more from me,
but that's all I can say. I'm still processing.
We head to the parking lot and wait for his parents
to pick us up and take us to his place.
It's Friday. And sometimes on Fridays,
I sleep at his house, or he sleeps at mine.

Dinner is simple.
Simple is quiet.
Peas and meat loaf
never started a riot.

Sammy's parents talk in a way
I thought only existed on-screen.
The Leave It to Beavers? The Cleavers?
The as-seen-on-TV-ers.
If this all sounds a bit uncomfortable,
it's because I was, I always am,
when I'm at Sammy's.

It's like his whole home is on mute.
His house is so — silent.

His parents are so — calm.
It's just — weird. I dunno.
Maybe it's normal.
But not at my house.
So whenever I'm at Sammy's, I try
to keep calm and quiet, because that seems
to be what people do around here.

His parents ask about Sammy's day at school,
about homework, and baseball practice.
They tell us about their day
at work (they work together)
at Raytheon.

Sammy's parents are smart.
Like, really smart.

Lots of people in Tucson work at Raytheon.
But not many of them can say
that they are literally
rocket scientists.

Sammy's parents can.
Sammy's parents build
things like rocket missiles
with epic names.

His mom says things at work are getting pretty busy.
Raytheon is making more of their most popular weapon,
the "Tomahawk."

That's a cool word.
"Is it named after a bird?" I ask.

"No, actually," his mom replies.
"A tomahawk was a Native American weapon,
similar to an axe."

"Not always, Sharon.
The tomahawk was a multipurpose tool,"
says Bill, Sammy's dad.

I wonder how many purposes
those missiles are going to have?
But I don't ask.

Can't any tool become a weapon?
Lots of things can be lots of things, I guess.
And lots of times they don't end up being
exactly the thing you thought they'd be.

I think that goes for families too.

Sammy is adopted. He's black.
Sammy's parents are white.
I'm sitting in between them,
trying to swallow
dry meat loaf.

Sammy finishes his food
and looks over at me to see if I'm done.
I am. He looks back at his parents and asks,
"Can we be excused?"

Blitz

In Sammy's room we play *Blitz 2000*
on his special-edition purple N64.

I'm the Buffalo Bills
(cuz Amir is obsessed with Doug Flutie,
and I kind of got into them too),
and Sammy is the Minnesota Vikings
(cuz Randy Moss).

Most of the guys at school play *Madden '01*,
a football video game that's so realistic,
it's almost like you're watching the real thing.
But I love *Blitz* because it's not that.
Blitz lets you run fast forever and break things.
Which surprisingly, I'm good at?
Sometimes even giving Sammy
a run for his money.

AND WE ARE UNDERWAY.

My go-to move is knocking out his receiver
as the digital ball is still soaring through the air,
then catching it with my defender,
who is already standing up
in the aftermath of the tackle.

MAKE THE INTERCEPTION.

Sammy calls it "pulling an Omid."
Sammy does that. Calls one thing
by another thing's name. Uses one word

where he should use another,
but the way he does it,
the sentence still
makes sense.

It's a Sammy superpower
if there ever was one.
My dad kinda has it too.
I'm stuck trying to find the right words
while they're off using the wrong ones
on purpose. And it's charming and
people love them for it.

They can bend language
like it's a wire hanger.

            ther   tool
        no   turn
      A   ed
                      w
                    e
               a
           p
           o
           n

Like using my name
like it's some kind of insult.
"Pulling an Omid!"

I don't really know what Omid means,
I admit that, but I'm pretty sure it's not some
terrible thing. I know I'm not some bad thing.

And I know Sammy knows that too,
cuz he's my best friend, and that's why
it makes me so mad when he just
changes what I mean.

"Pulling an Omid!"
Like it's some cheap move.
Well, if it was so cheap, how come
the game lets me do it?
Celebrates it, even!
How come it
feels so
good?

Interception

It's not a cheap move.
Sammy just hates losing.

I Win Our First Game, A Rare Feat

"If you're gonna keep that Omid shit up,
then I'm switching teams.
No one does Randy Moss like that,"
Sammy threatens.

"If you're so scared, switch then."
I call his bluff
as the guitars from
Green Day's "Brain Stew"
begin to blare in my mind.

"Fine. Colts it is. Let's see you deal with Edgerrin."

Cymbals crash, and now the drums are playing too,
in my head, as I'm trying to hype
myself up for this rematch.

Key word: trying. It's not really working.

I must've gotten under Sammy's skin.
He hasn't played with anyone but the Vikings in months.
I got cocky. If I'm being honest, I don't know
how to defend against the running game.

This might have been a mistake.

Sammy switches teams while my body does that thing
where my heart beats quicker than it should,
and I feel like I'm about to start sweating.
It's just a video game. I know that.
But I feel like he's angry with me.

I feel like everything
is about to go
wrong.

I know what might make me feel better.

"You mind?"
I take Emily's CD out of my backpack
and flash it at Sammy as I walk over
to the silver Sony boom box in the corner.

I hold it up long enough for him to see what it is
but not long enough for him to see what's on it.
No need for him to see the tiny hearts drawn
instead of dots above the *i*'s
in *Omid's Mix*.

"Whaaat? You brought music?! Since when?"
"Since today."
"Well, well, well, okay! Throw it on."

It Takes Three Songs

before Sammy even mentions it.
His Colts are up by twenty-one over my Bills.
So he speaks with authority.
"What the hell is this?"
"I'm still adjusting, rewarming up."
"No, I mean your music. It's trash."

Heart sinking quick —
if he doesn't like it,
why do I?

No.
Stop. I gotta try
to kick this sidekick habit.

"Yeah, well, I like it."
"Really? Where'd you get it?"

Caught.

"Why's that matter?" I ask.
"It matters cuz we've been friends for like ever
and you've never really listened to music
and now you do?"

Okay, it's safe to say my hype tracks
aren't working out as planned. I don't know
what to say. Sammy goes on,
"And it matters cuz two dudes sitting in a room
listening to Dashboard Confessional
is kinda . . . lame."

Sammy tends to know things I don't,
like band names and what not
to do if you want to be cool.

"Well — I don't think it's lame —
cuz I got it from a girl."
"Oh, oh, Omid!
What?! Why didn't you say so?
This changes everything."

He pauses the game to grill me
right before I'm finally about to score.

Then I Tell

Sammy about Emily.

I tell him
not because I owe him an explanation,
but because I have this feeling
that has grown so huge and heavy
that I need to get it off my chest
and out of my head
and into someone else's.

I need to know what Sammy knows.
I need — help.

See, we've done this before.
Had these talks, about girls.
But I've always been on the other side.
Not talking much but listening
to Sammy talk about Monica,
or Rachel, or Jenna, or Kate.
Nodding along as Sammy strategized,
wishing I knew how he
gets those girls
to like him.

But Emily isn't just some girl
like Monica, or Rachel, or Jenna, or Kate.
Emily is different, for me.

I feel like we are friends,
or maybe more than friends, or maybe more
than more than friends. Maybe there are no words

for what we are. Yet. But I am gonna try to find them.

First attempt:
"She's really dope, I mean, *really* dope."

Second attempt:
"When we talk . . . it's different."

Third attempt:
"I just think she's — special — you know?"

And I would have kept swinging,
but Sammy recognizes a strikeout when he sees it.

That's What Friends Are For

"Chillax, bro. I get it.
You're into this girl."
"Uh, yeah, sure — that covers it."

Does it, though?

"But that's still no excuse
to bring Bright Eyes into my house.
If you're gonna start listening to music,
at least treat yourself to the best.
And lucky for you, you've got me
to make you a mix with some songs
that will change your life . . ."

I needed help. I needed
to know what Sammy knew
about girls. But instead,
I'm getting another CD.

Sammy looks like he's getting
something out of this too,
but I'm not exactly sure
what it is.

He's so excited
to share his music with me, like it might
actually help me, like it might have
actually helped him, like it might have
made his life better.

I wonder what Sammy wants.

Not for me, but for himself.
In all the years we've been friends,
we've never really talked about that.
But I don't think we're about to start now,
so I just say, "Sweet. Yeah, that'd be cool. Thanks, man."

"That's what friends are for."

He smirks a Sammy smile and unpauses our game
as I fumble the ball on the ten-yard line.

In The Guest Bedroom

That's where I'm supposed to sleep
when I'm staying the night
at Sammy's house.

And I do.

Because if there's a whole bedroom in a house
dedicated to the guest — and YOU are that guest —
then not sleeping in that bedroom would be rude, right?

That would be, like, the opposite of *tarof*.
And as much as I don't like *tarof*,
I would never not *tarof*
in a *tarof*-worthy
situation.

Except.

I don't exactly love
sleeping alone. Not yet anyway.
I mean, I shared a bedroom with my brother
for most of my life. Maybe after I've had my own
for a little while longer, maybe then I'll be different.
But right now it still feels wrong.

Not wrong.
But really weird.
Which is actually what Sammy says too
whenever my mom makes him a makeshift mattress
in my room on the Friday nights he sleeps over at our place.
He says it's really weird. Then he'll just wait

till he's really tired, or Amir and I are falling asleep,
to take his pillow and his blanket down to the living room
and sleep on the couch.

I tried that once at his house too.

Kind of.

We'd said good night. I went to the guest room
but couldn't sleep cuz I felt uncomfortable.
So I got up, with my pillow and blanket in hand,
but instead of heading to the couch in the living room —
I went to Sammy's room
and slept on the floor.

It was the fastest I've ever fallen asleep at his house.
Maybe it's an Iranian thing, where we just try
to keep our family and friends as close as possible.
Or maybe I was just comfortable. I don't know.

But the next morning, when Sammy woke up
and saw me on his floor, the first thing he said
was, "Yo, dude — what are you doing in here?"

And — I lied. I said something about
wanting to play more N64
after he fell asleep and
how I must have passed out
without realizing it.

Sammy listened to my story.
Sammy saw my blanket and my pillow.
But Sammy didn't say anything.

That was cool of him.

I haven't done that since.
Eventually, I found a way to fall asleep
in the guest room.

If you just try to keep your eyes open
for as long as you can and try to see everything you can
even though it's really dark, but you just keep trying, keep
looking, never closing your eyes, they might start to hurt,
but you just keep them open until there are tears
rolling down your cheeks and you tell yourself,

"I'm not crying.
I'm just not blinking"

over and over until the white ceiling in the room
starts to look like a black ceiling and then starts to look
like a white ceiling again and there's no more water left
in your eyes, then just like that you're asleep.

A Real Character

Mr. Thompson asked Ms. Lowell
to ask me to go see him
at lunch.

"Thanks for dropping by, Omid.
I'm going to put up the cast list today after school,
but before I do, I wanted to chat with you . . ."

"Is everything okay?"

"Oh yeah, 'course it is!
Sorry. I didn't mean to worry you.
Just wanted to have a moment
where we could get to know
each other better!

You see, I've been making theater for a long time —
directing, acting, even writing some when I was younger.
And I haven't always lived in Tucson —
I spent decades in New York City.

You know, I probably directed
some of your favorite actors
when they were just a little
older than you are now."

I didn't know why
Mr. Thompson was telling me about New York City.
I'd never been asked to go to see a teacher at lunch,
I don't think, especially not a teacher
whose class I wasn't even taking.

I couldn't shake the feeling
that I was in trouble
for something.

"This is all to say:

You're a very talented kid, Omid. You're a natural.

And I know — I know you
probably want to play one of the lovers,
because all kids your age want to play lovers,
and you really did have a great audition with Emily,
but I'd like for you to play a character —
a real character — that's big enough
to hold all your talent.

Nick Bottom could give you that opportunity.

You'd have more room to play, to create, and to experiment,
than you'd ever have if I cast you as Demetrius or Lysander,"
he said.

"Would you do that for me, Omid?
Would you play Bottom?"
he said.

You're a very talented kid, Omid.

He said.

You're a natural.

To Be Natural

is to be normal.

To be normal

would be amazing.

"Of course, Mr. Thompson . . .
I'd love to."

The Cast List

went up outside the theater doors at 3:15 p.m.

Athenians

Theseus	Mike Bend
Hippolyta	Maria Morales
Egeus	Jamie Garrison
Philostrate	David Lawrence

Lovers

Hermia	Emily Bishop
Lysander	Geoff Sterling
Demetrius	Robbie Robeson
Helena	Kate Kornicki

Fairies

Oberon	Jamal Washington
Titania	Sarah Powers
Puck	Natalie Sampson
Peaseblossom	Shayna Carr
Mustardseed	Monica Rosen
Moth	Jessica Tam
Cobweb	Abby Valentina

Mechanicals

Rita Quince	Rebecca Brooks
Nick Bottom	Omid Soltani
Francis Flute	Javier De Leon
Robin Starveling	Douglas South
Tom Snout	Tomas Vargas
Snug	Nate Ferguson

Overthinking It

"Nick Bottom. Omid Soltani."
A real character. Big enough
to hold all that talent.

What does that even mean?
What makes one character
any realer than another?
How big does something have to be
to be able to hold all of . . . me?

Playing Bottom feels so good.

But it also means
I can't be a lover
with Emily.

Maybe I should have said no?

Maybe I should have told
Mr. Thompson the truth,
that Bottom was fantastic,
but I still really wanted
to be a lover.

I think I messed up.
I think I missed my chance.
I think I'm overthinking it.

I should be celebrating.
I should be heading home, head held high.
I should be carrying myself with confidence.

Instead, I'm riffling through my script,
rife with worry about a kiss
between Hermia and Lysander.

Do they ever?

Of course they do.
Right?

What kind of story would this be
if the lovers never kissed?

But I can't find it.
Not in the dialogue
or the stage directions.

Now there's nothing I can do but wait and see
what Mr. Thompson asks
of Geoff Sterling
and Emily.

Together

I was sitting on the brick wall
by parent pickup, waiting for my mom,
when Emily ran up to me, beaming.

"We're going to be in *Midsummer* — together!"
"Yeah!" I tried to sound excited about it. I really did.
"You're going to be an awesome Hermia."
"YOU got Bottom, Omid! He's, like . . . the lead mechanical!
I'm so proud of you."

"Yeah, thanks," I said as I tried really super hard
not to think about her kissing Geoff Sterling.

                                        Fun fact:

                                        the best way
                            to definitely think about something
                                is to try hard not to think about it.

So as I tried not to think about, but definitely thought about,
Emily kissing Geoff, she said,

"By the way, when we first talked
by the lockers the other day,
I might have lied a little.
I didn't actually know
who Tracy Chapman was."

"What?! You called it old-people music!"

"I know. I know! But I listened to her album,

and I actually really like her!
That song 'Fast Car' — it's so beautiful."

Then she put her arm around my shoulder and said,
"Sorry I called it old-people music.
I guess your taste isn't *all* bad."

And my heart beat a little bit faster.
Because I really liked that
Emily really liked her.
I really liked
her too.

Cliché

Emily makes me feel a way
I've never felt before.

And I know that's a cliché.
But can something be cliché
if it's true?

There's something about
the way she looks at me and
waits for me to see her
and *then* smiles
that makes me want,
more than anything,
to be whatever
she wants me
to be.

That makes me need,
more than anything,
to be whatever
she needs me
to be.

But as hard as I try —
and believe me, I'm trying —
I don't know what that is.

Because I just can't imagine
Emily *needing*
anything.

Sir

We were going to get groceries.
I was sitting in the passenger seat
as Mom parked the car.
She opened her door,
when tires howled,
an engine growled,
and a Ford truck zoomed
into the space on our left.

Mom threw her legs back into the car
and held the door close to her body.
We waited
until the night
blue truck was still,
its engine off,
the growl gone,
the creature asleep,
and got out of our car.

Something felt wrong.
But something always feels wrong,
so I tried to ignore it.

I speed-walked past the truck,
but Mom took her time.

"Be careful the next time you come in here that fast,"
she said, over her shoulder,
to the man as he got out of his truck.

"There are kids around."

I don't understand why
she had to say anything at all.
We were walking to the store.
We could have left
the growling
behind us.

The man yelled after her.

"What did you say to me?
You almost hit my truck with your door, lady!"
His voice was fuller than his frail frame implied.

"Oh, please!
I had already parked
and was trying to get out of my car."
My mom lobbed her words
back toward him over an invisible net
like she was playing tennis,
a game she knew so well
she could play it with her eyes closed.

The man's voice got louder.
"Look at me when you talk to me,
you crazy Arab bitch."

A dog barked.
No.
My mom.
My mom barked.

I spun around to see
a man's face inches from hers

a man's hand gripping the top of her shirt
a man shaking her as she tried to pull away.

And then,

"Excuse me . . . sir,"
I said.
Not moving.
Not breathing.
Not speaking.

Was I really speaking?

The man looked at me.
He heard my words
unencumbered
by the weight
of an accent.

He saw my knees
shaking
almost as hard
as my voice.

"She didn't mean it,"
I said,
having used up all
my oxygen
on
seven
words.

He stared at me.
He let go of her.
He turned around.
He walked into the store.

We ran
back into our car.
We locked the doors.
We felt awful,
awful sick,
and sweaty,
lucky to be
breathing
heavy

as we realized we should leave, quick,
before he came back from his grocery trip.

We drove home
silent.

It started to rain.

Creosote In The Rain

There is a smell, seemingly sprouting from the sands
after Sonoran Desert rains, that soaks the air.
It sits in small pockets of breath
and slides down your lungs and
slows down your brain,
reminding you to stop
and smell the roses.

Or, in this case, the creosote bush.

A desert shrub that can live for millennia,
and can go two years without a drink of water.
A soft plant made tough by circumstance.
It survives the dangers of the Arizona desert
by coating its leaves and yellow flowers with a wax
that protects it from the sun's heat. That wax
tastes awful to potential predators
but smells something special when it's wet.

After it rains, the plant's aroma takes over the desert.

It smells fresh.
But not like the fresh we find bottled
and sold in aerosol cans.
It smells like relief.
But a relief you could only feel
when you're drinking rain
after two long years
of thirst.

It smells like freedom.

But a freedom you could only know
if you lived in a hard, hot world,
a world that might even want you dead,
and yet, somehow

you are still alive.

Maman Joon

hugs me hard,
like she does each time
we step inside her home.

The longer we have known each other,
the longer our hugs have gotten.
The longer our hugs have gotten, the more I start to believe
this is her way of telling me how much she loves me.

She holds me tight and sways us both
from side to side. My mom's mom feels safe.
And solid. And full of everything
a parent should be
full of.

Maman Joon
doesn't try to strike up
conversation the way Baba Joon
does. Doesn't drag us on hikes to the outskirts
of our comfort zones. She is comfortable
being together without all that.
She is comfortable being
without words even.

She is cooking tonight.
She is always cooking,
        always trying
        to fill our plates,
        to never leave us
        empty.

We Never Told Dad

about what happened in the parking lot at the grocery store.

And now I'm realizing
Mom isn't going to tell
Maman Joon or Baba Joon
or maybe anyone else at all.

Because we've arrived at the last course
of this Sunday night *mehmooni* at my grandparents' place,
and my aunt Simin is visiting from Phoenix,
and she's telling us a story about Sahbah, her husband,
and something that someone said to him
at work about what happened in New York.

Apparently his coworkers wanted him to translate
something they'd found on the internet about the terrorists,
which was in Arabic, and Sahbah had to explain to them
that he didn't speak Arabic, he spoke Farsi,
and while the two do share an alphabet,
the languages are definitely different.

Persians and Arabs might be from the same part of the planet,
but they aren't the same people. Simin is telling us
how Sahbah's friends didn't believe him,
how one of the guys even said,

"I bet he knows exactly what this says,
he just doesn't want to tell us."

Something about that guy in Simin's story
reminds me of that guy in the parking lot,

and I think it's the perfect time
for Mom to tell everyone
what happened.

But she doesn't.

Instead she just says,

*"That's really terrible, Simin jan.
Oh, by the way, did I tell you all Omid's big news?
He was cast in the school play!"*

Which feels like a pretty hard tangent to everyone there —
but since Amir is already asleep in the other room
and I'm the only kid still actively trying to *mehmooni*,
they want me to feel included,
so they congratulate me.

Maman Joon even asks, *"Which play are you in, azizam?"*

And I start to think
about how I would even begin to translate
the title *A Midsummer Night's Dream* into Farsi.

But Mom says something right away,
while I'm thinking hard about translating,
so I don't catch it all, and it sounds like Persian gibberish,
but there is one word that jumps out, above the others,
kind of like this:

                       Shakespeare
"gibberish gibberish gibberish   gibberish gibberish"

And then Baba Joon says something
I never even thought was possible.

"How wonderful!
I love Mr. Shakespeare!
I read the translations in college."

Baba Joon has read Shakespeare in Farsi???
How is that possible?! Which was his favorite?!

But before I can find out,
Dad comes into the room with
Amir half sleepwalking behind him.

"Shohreh, Omid, come. I think it's time we
get Amir home. Thank you all so much
for the lovely evening."

And then everyone gets up and starts kissing each other,
and I don't even rush that part this time,
because I feel like I'm floating again,
like I did at my audition, and I just can't wait
for the day Baba Joon sees me
in a Shakespeare play.

Our Stories, Old Stories

When we got home,
I did something I've never done before.
I called Baba Joon on the phone.

And I was scared.

Which might sound silly to say,
but what I had to do wasn't as simple as calling
any old friend on the phone. I had to assemble
a conversation in Farsi without the glue
of body language. Which, for all intents
and purposes, was like riding a bike
without training wheels. No. It was even worse.
It was like riding a bike with only one wheel.
I had to ride a unicycle, so to speak.

Calling my grandparents
felt like a circus act.

So yeah—I was scared. But I did it anyway
because now I knew something
Baba Joon and I both liked,
now we had another thing to share,
and maybe that would be enough . . .
maybe that could change everything.

The phone rang twice, and he picked up.
I spoke, in my broken Farsi.
"Hi, Baba Joon! It's Omid.
Which Shakespeare you read?"

I could tell he was happy
to hear from me. He spoke vigorously,
saying so many words I didn't understand.
But I did manage to catch the title of one play,
because it was made up of just two names,
and names don't change as you travel
from one language into another.
"*Romeo va Juliet.*"

Baba Joon had read a translation of *Romeo and Juliet* in Farsi.

That's so cool.

I asked him why he liked it,
and he said, in broken English,
"Shakespeare, he know Iran!"

I was surprised — and confused.
Which he must have felt through the phone,
because he went back to Farsi, all the way back
to a simple Farsi he knew I could follow, and explained:
"*Shakespeare must have been a very smart man,
because he knows the history, he knows the poetry, of Iran!
This story is taken from our stories.
From our poets. From our past.*

*Layli and Majnun, by Nezami Ganjavi.
You must read it, Omid. It is our story
of two young loves that die
when they cannot be together.*

*Here is Romeo and Juliet before Romeo and Juliet.
Here is Shakespeare before Shakespeare.*"

New Stories

When I said I can't wait for the day
Baba Joon sees me in the play,
I meant I can't wait for the day
Baba Joon sees ME in the play.

I like to think whenever someone tells a story,
even an old one, they put a piece
of themselves inside it.

And that piece
makes the whole
thing new.

Baba Joon said that Persian story, *Layli and Majnun*,
was *Romeo and Juliet* before *Romeo and Juliet* . . .
was Shakespeare before Shakespeare . . .
But was it really?

Like when Shakespeare told his version
of the Persian tale, he changed it. Filled it in
with shades of him. Made it something different.

And when I'm playing Bottom . . .
It's kind of like I'm doing
the same thing?

I might be using Shakespeare's words,
sure, but HE isn't there saying them.
That part is me. That part
is me. I think.
Maybe?

Act One, Scene Two

We're rehearsing my first scene in the show today.

Act one, scene two.
Where Bottom is trying
to convince Quince to let him play
pretty much every part in the script.

This one is fun. Because I get to be
as ridiculous as I can be, pretending
I'm a lady
     and a tyrant
               and a lover
                        and a lion,
because the joke of this scene is
that Bottom isn't so much *good* at acting
as much as he *wants* to be good at acting.

I love this scene
because it lets me try
anything and everything
that comes to mind. It lets me show
people all the places
I can go.

And because this is the scene I auditioned with.

This is the scene I did so well that
Mr. Thompson called me
a natural.

Sneaking Off Into The Woods During Rehearsal

Everything in me is saying: don't do it.

There are rules
against this kind of thing.
Against leaving campus during school.
But everyone hangs out outside
when they aren't onstage,
and I guess *after* school
isn't *during* school.

Rehearsal is such a gray area.

"We shouldn't go, Em. I think
it's against the rules. What if
we get caught? What if
we get into trouble?
Is it really worth it?"

But she wants to go.

"Nothing is going to happen, Omid. The park is literally
around the corner. We'll all jump in Geoff's car and
be back before they're done with the Oberon/Titania scene.
I don't want to go without you. Please?"

There are rules
against this kind of thing.
Against me getting into a car
not driven by a parent I know.
Mom and Dad would be pissed.
But Mom and Dad aren't here.

They don't know
how this feels.

Emily looks confused. Almost defeated.
Like she lost something she thought she had.
She sighs. She turns around and walks back
toward the theater, but not before saying:

"I wish you weren't so worried all the time."

And that's when I'm struck with a thought, like lightning.
Maybe this is what Emily needs from me?
To ignore my gut and all my old ways.
To follow my heart and take a leap
of faith for her. With her.

"No — you're right. It's not that big of a deal.

Let's go."

Cool

We're all squeezing into the back seat
of Geoff's car, which smells like a big shoe
filled with flowers. Legs on laps.
People searching for seat belts.

I was wrong.

This feels dumb, and smart people don't do dumb things,
and I thought Emily was smarter than this.
I thought I was smarter than this.

In the park, a fire burns between her lips.
Something small can feel so big.
They're all smoking cigarettes, and
Emily is smoking a cigarette, and I'm sweating,
confused, defeated, like I lost something I thought I had.
I'm dizzy. I look at the ground. I try not to lose
my balance.

I wanted to be close enough to her to smell her,
but I never thought she would smell like this.
And now, somehow, I'm starting to miss everything
that came before this. Even the stupid flower shoe
and the feeling of legs on laps and everyone
searching for some way
to feel safe.

Geoff and some of the other seniors start to laugh,
so I smile and even laugh loudly at jokes that aren't funny
just to remind people I exist at this picnic table
conference of cool.

It's A Good Thing Too

It's Friday, so I head over to the baseball field
after rehearsal is out. Tonight
I sleep at Sammy's house.
It's a good thing too,
cuz where there's fire
there's smoke, and I smell
like smoke, and I don't
know what kind of fire
I'd start if I had to go
straight home
to Mom.

Pretty Pale

"You okay, dude?"
Sammy asks me as he stuffs baseball bats
into a big bag in the dugout.
"Yeah, why?"
"You look pretty pale."
"I do? No, I'm good."
"Alright, if you say so.

Listen, I gotta drop this stuff off
and grab my backpack from the locker room.
We're gonna catch a ride home in Sean's car.
You can head over and meet him in the parking lot."
"Who's Sean?"
"Our third baseman. No worries, he's solid.
My folks are working late so they can't pick us up.
But they left money for pizza."

I'm not supposed to get into a car unless a parent
I know is driving it. Mom and Dad even said
I could call them anytime I needed a ride,
and they'd be there to pick me up, no questions asked.
They said I'd never get into trouble for calling them.

But I smell like smoke.
And I already broke their rule once today, for Emily.
Might as well do it again, for Sammy.

Besides, once a rule is broken,
what's the point in putting
it back together?

Fear Factor

We order a large Domino's pizza to split.

Meat lovers, cuz Sammy is back to eating bread
as long as he can pack on the protein. And I'm always
looking for an excuse to eat pepperoni or sausage,
cuz we never have it at home.

Sammy says he's too tired to play *Blitz* tonight,
so we throw on a TiVoed episode of *Fear Factor*.
It's the one where the contestants have to jump
out of a hotel window and hold on to a trapeze bar
before falling 120 feet to the ground
before eating sheep's eyeballs
before holding their breath
upside down in a tank
of water, for a prize.

I don't understand
why they'd do all that
for fifty thousand dollars.
It really grosses me out,
but Sammy seems to like it.

"So you gonna tell me why you reek of cigarettes, or
are we just gonna keep pretending that you don't?"

This is unexpected. Maybe because I honestly forgot about it
as soon as the pizza arrived. Maybe because
I didn't expect Sammy to care,
because I know Sammy has friends who smoke,
and it's just another thing we don't talk about.

But he asked me —
and there's really no reason to lie to Sammy.

"I went to the park with Emily during rehearsal.
Her and this guy Geoff and some of his friends.
They smoked, but I didn't. So yeah. No big deal."

"You sure about that?"

"Am I sure about what?"

"That it's
no big deal."

A Tornado Made Of Words Sammy Said Next

you can't just
              bullshit me
                          like that
                                    it's not like
                                                 I don't know you, Omid.
anytime   anyone   ever
              wanted to smoke
or wanted to drink

                                                                    last year
         you bailed out the room so hard, it made us wonder

    what the hell just happened?

                                         should we be worried?
  but now
      you
          (you!)
               you are into some chick
                              who smokes cigs in the park

             and burns you
                           god-awful CDs

          she
              sounds like
              a bad
                   influence,
                   to me.

I Can Hear The Difference

I knew Sammy was trying to sound mad.
But he wasn't mad.
He was hurt.

I can tell, sometimes,
when people are hurting.

It's not what they say.
It's how they say it.

When people are mad,
they sound like they're about to burst.
When people are hurting,
they sound like they're about to break.

To most people, those two things sound the same.
But I can hear the difference.

Sammy was about to break.
I'm not sure why,
but I could hear it.
So I said the only thing
that made sense to say:

"I'm sorry."

Then Sammy surprised me.
He took a moment. And then,
he almost said it back.
In his own way.

"Nah. I'm just playing with you, dude.
Just use my shower real quick
before my parents get home.
I'll give you some fresh clothes."

And after a few more seconds of neither of us knowing
what to say to the other, Sammy spoke again.
"It's good. We're all good."

Good, Part 2

In the shower
I can't stop thinking.

About Emily in the park.
About the man in the parking lot.
About rehearsal and about the play.

About the fire.
About *Fear Factor*.
About my old ways.

About the new me,
the news on TV, Sammy,
and my family.

Are we?

Are we all good?

Sammy's CD

Sammy left me clothes on the bed in the guest room.
Beside the gym shorts and tee, I see something else, a burned CD.
There's a note taped to the bottom of the case.

Definition — Black Star
The Way I Am — Eminem
Renegade — Jay-Z (ft. Eminem)
Can I Kick It? — A Tribe Called Quest
Check the Rhime — A Tribe Called Quest
Doo Wop (That Thing) — Ms. Lauryn Hill
B.O.B. (Bombs Over Baghdad) — Outkast
Country Grammar (Hot Shit) — Nelly
Hate Me Now — Nas (ft. Puff Daddy)
Get Ur Freak On — Missy Elliott
Changes — 2Pac
Rosa Parks — Outkast
Hypnotize — The Notorious B.I.G.
Bad Boy for Life — P. Diddy
Hard Knock Life (Ghetto Anthem) — Jay-Z
Money Ain't a Thang — Jermaine Dupri (ft. Jay-Z)

Better than Bright Eyes. You're welcome.
— Sammy

Switching Sides

Emily is on the phone again
and wants to know what I think.
"Do you think I should go?"

But first, a history.
Our history.
How this all started
with history homework.

It's Saturday.
The two of us have been talking a lot
on Saturdays.
See, I might have once casually mentioned
that I placed into AP US History, knowing Emily didn't,
knowing Emily struggled with history.
Since then, she's started calling me
anytime she's needed help.

Today we're talking about the ramifications of Reconstruction.

I'm trying to explain
how President Andrew Johnson declared victory,
claimed his mission accomplished, perhaps preemptively,
claimed Reconstruction complete, and slavery solved,
despite tons of objections and concrete evidence
of lingering oppression.

I'm trying to explain
how this paved a path for more partisanship,
how the Radical Republicans pushed back hard,
how they fought for the rights of the former slaves.

When Emily suddenly stops me.
"Wait. Radical Republicans?
I thought the Democrats
fought for civil rights in the South."

She's right.
Kind of.
"Oh yeah, they did!
But that was like
a hundred years later.
Which is plenty of time
for sides to switch.
The parties aren't exactly
what they used to be."
"Yeah, I guess not.
So speaking of parties, have you — "
But then her voice goes silent.
"Have I what?"
"No, never mind. It's so not related to this.
It's nothing, really."
"That's okay. What's up?"

"It's just that — well — Geoff
is having a party next weekend.
It's at his house and he invited me
after rehearsal. After we all got back
from the park. And I didn't expect it.
And I don't know.

Do you think I should go?"

Oh.
Whoa.

Okay. Emily wants to know what I think.
How do I say, "Please don't go"
without actually saying, "Please don't go"?
"Well — do you want to?"

"I think so. I mean, we've got a lot of scenes together
in the show, and I don't really know him. Wouldn't it be good
to spend more time together?"
"I mean, I think your scenes are fine.
Totally great, actually. You don't have to go
just because you're in the show with him."
"I knew you'd say that."

How did she know I'd say that?
I didn't even know I'd say that.

"But I guess it's not just because of the show.
I mean, I'm still new at Nova. You and Sarah
are like my only friends right now, Omid.
It would be nice to meet people
outside of class."

What do I say to that?
Are Sarah and I not good enough for you, Emily?
Or am I just trying to keep you all to myself?

Why did Geoff invite her anyway?
Am I being selfish?
I'm being selfish.

And I'm always worried. We've covered that. What if
I just didn't worry about Emily? What's the worst
that could happen?

Just then she says,
"Omid. Would you go with me?"
"Go where?"
"To Geoff's party."

I don't tell her I wasn't invited.
I don't tell her I'd rather
take her somewhere,
anywhere else, just the two of us.
And I especially don't tell her
she's only doing all those scenes
with Geoff because of *me*,
because Mr. Thompson thinks I'm a natural,
and he so asked me *not* to play Lysander
and to play Bottom instead.

I don't say any of that.
I can't. Instead, I just try
to sound — busy. Unattached.
And absolutely not jealous.

"No. Sorry. I can't. I've already got plans with Sammy."

My Excuse

lasted three whole days.

Until I heard the whole varsity baseball team
got invites to Geoff's party.

And since Sammy made varsity, that includes him.
I don't think Sammy's ever said no to a party . . .
so he's definitely gonna go.

Now what do I do?

Scared, Part 2

Today at lunch Sammy asked
if I had listened to his CD yet.
"Not yet, dude, but I will soon."

We sat and ate in silence
as Sammy sorta stewed, and I slowly built up the nerve
to ask him if he was gonna go to Geoff's party.

"Probably, yeah,"
he said, in a way that made it obvious
that this wasn't some big decision for him.
In a way that made me feel stupid
for even asking.

No. Not stupid.
Something similar,
but much stronger.

Scared.

Scared that my two best friends
would leave me behind,
courted by the upperclassmen,
all confident and cool at Geoff's house,
scared that they would fit in
and forget to look back.

"Emily got invited too."
"The CD girl? From the play?"
"Yeah. Apparently, Geoff invited her
after we went to that park last week."

"That makes sense."
It does?
"Yeah — well, she's invited —
and you're invited —
and I'm not —
so what do I do?"
"Dude. If you want to come, just come."
"I can't. No one invited me."
"You're stressing about this invite thing, Omid.
No one is like checking names at the door.
There's gonna be a ton of people there.
You can just tag along with me if you want."

If I want.

If only I knew
what I wanted.

I didn't want to go. But I wanted to go too.
I wanted to see Emily. But I didn't want to see Geoff.
I hated how I felt around him in the park. But I still wanted
to see her. I wanted two things, too many things, at once.
I didn't want to go. But I wanted to go too.

"Don't make such a big deal out of it, man.
Just tell your parents you're sleeping at my house on Friday
and catch a ride to the party with Sean and me."

Sammy's confidence is amazing.

More than anything, I wanted to be like that.

"Okay. Sounds good."

The Top Of Act Three

We're running the top of act three at rehearsal today.

It's our first time rehearsing the mechanicals' first rehearsal
in the forest outside Athens. In the same forest where Oberon,
the king of the fairies, has quarreled with wife, Titania,
and has instructed his henchman, Puck, to put her
under a spell that will make her fall in love
with the very first thing she sees.

Oberon seems to be the kind of king
who prefers pranks over apologies.

So when Puck hears Bottom performing loudly
with his troupe, he waits till no one's looking
and gives Bottom the head of a donkey.
Then, when the newly minted man-meets-mule
scares off all the other actors, Puck leads Bottom
into the sleeping queen's lair,
where she promptly falls
in love with him.

It's a big moment for me. A big sequence
with Omid right in the middle.

And to stage it, we need
pretty much everyone in
the cast. Except for the lovers.
So, pretty much everyone is here . . .

Except for Emily.

The theater is full but
somehow feels empty
without her.

I don't like the feeling of her missing. Of missing her.
I try to distract myself with lines, or blocking,
or anything at all.

I pretend to be Bottom, I pretend to be Bottom pretending
to be Pyramus. I pretend to be oblivious.
And at the point where I'm pretending
to be half-dude half-donkey,
Rebecca, playing Quince,
sees me and shouts,

                    "Bless thee, Bottom, Bless thee!
                        Thou art translated!"

and I can't get it out of my head.

In this scene, where Bottom looks like a literal ass,
unknowingly terrifying all of his closest friends,
Shakespeare wrote *not* that he was transformed,
but that he was . . . "translated"!

Why . . . would Shakespeare . . . do that?

All The World's A Stage

NIGHT.

Upstairs: AMIR is asleep.

*Downstairs: OMID is on the sofa, writing in the journal
BABA JOON gave him. He's thinking about rehearsal today and
GEOFF's party tomorrow and SAMMY's plan. OMID is nervous.
He's going to have to lie to his parents. He hates lying. But he loves
acting. He wonders — would this all be easier if he just thought
of lying as acting? MOM is in the kitchen, clanking and cleaning
dishes. OMID feels the garage door rumble open from across the
house. A few seconds pass, then DAD enters. DAD is home late,
again. He sits on the sofa next to OMID.*

MOM brings DAD a plate of food.

They speak in Farsi.

MOM
Here you go. By the way, Richard from the bank called.

DAD
Yeah? Okay, thanks, dear.

MOM
He said you can call him back tonight. It sounded important.

DAD starts eating.

MOM
Is everything okay?

DAD
What? Yeah. Of course it is. I'm just tired.
I'll call him tomorrow.

MOM
You know, I've been meaning to say,
since my mom and dad are settled in
and you're finally in the new store . . .
I can always go back.

DAD attempts a joke.

DAD
Go back? Where? To Iran?

MOM
Very funny, you idiot.

OMID notices that the word for "idiot" in Farsi is "khar."

MOM
I meant back to real estate.

*OMID realizes that "khar," when translated into English
literally, means "donkey."*

DAD
Why would you do that?

MOM
To help. Why not? If we need
a little extra — for the new loan.

OMID imagines DAD translated, transformed,
with the head of an ass.

DAD
Eh! Just stop that. No. November is coming up,
and November is always good. Thanksgiving.
Everyone redecorates! Everyone buys rugs!

MOM squints, unsatisfied.
DAD's voice softens.

DAD
Really, my love. You don't have to worry.
There's nothing to worry about.

MOM
I'm not worrying. I'm offering.
You know, I wasn't supposed to stop working forever.
We just got busy, distracted, with everything this summer.

DAD
This conversation is over! We don't need it. I don't want you —
in your car with strangers — showing property —
alone — these days.

MOM
Oh you don't? Not these days?
Who's worried now?

MOM drops it and walks away. DAD turns on the TV and starts
to watch the news. OMID closes his journal, walks upstairs, and
falls asleep in bed.

Into The Cookie Jar

When we got to Geoff's house,
it was one surprise after another.
First of all, his parents were there.
Why'd I think they'd be out of town?

They were most definitely not out of town.
They were most definitely in the kitchen.
And they were pretty nice, actually.

They said hi to each of us and asked everyone
to put their car keys into the cookie jar.
A cookie jar they would keep
in their bedroom until morning,
so we couldn't leave,
until they let us.

And everyone just did it. Everyone was cool with it,
because it meant Geoff's parents were cool with us
doing whatever we wanted to do until then, I guess?
I'd never been to a party like this.

There were some other parents there, too.
But I didn't recognize any of them.
I didn't recognize anyone

except Emily.

Emily. Who saw us in the kitchen and ran over right away,
gave me a hug, and said, "Omid! I'm so glad
you guys decided to come . . . I was starting to worry
Sarah and I would be the only sophomores here."

A Mutant Bird

The next surprise was the size.

My house is big. It's the biggest house in our family for sure,
so I always assumed I had it good.
But Geoff's house was huge.

Like big enough that it didn't have rooms,
it had wings. And not just two wings like a normal bird,
it had four wings, like a mutant bird.
East Wing and West Wing and North Wing and South Wing.

Geoff lived in the South Wing,
in an attached guesthouse
that could have been a whole home
if his courtyard were a kitchen.
That's where we all were sitting,
in Geoff's room, on Geoff's couch,
on Geoff's beanbags, on Geoff's floor.

There was pizza and PlayStation present.
A *Madden* tournament was mid-round
when some of the senior girls asked if
anyone wanted to go swimming.

I felt like Sammy and I could get into this tournament,
but I didn't want Emily to feel left out
(plus if you "pull an Omid" in *Madden*
you get called for a penalty).

Just then, a group of senior boys came into the room
through the sliding glass door from the courtyard.

"You guys smell that?"
I said, breathing in a gross muddy melting smell.
"Close the door. I think there's a skunk out there."

Geoff shot up off the couch and rushed to the door,
and then he looked at his friends,
and then he looked at me,
and then he started to laugh,
and then his friends started to laugh,
so I just started laughing too.

But to be honest, I'm starting to feel like
I never really know why Geoff is laughing.

Skunked

"It's weed, bro. That smell is weed,"

Sammy told me,
as the skunked senior boys
huddled up with the *Madden* crowd.

Rope

"How did Sammy know that?"
I thought.
I thought it a lot.

He's always been two steps ahead.
A natural fit at fitting in.

Sammy always had an answer.
For his parents.
For his team.
For me.

And I've always had my suspicions
that Sammy drank or smoked
or toked or whatever it took
to climb the social ladder.

It's actually one of the things I like most about him.

Sammy strives.

Too bad he's no good,
or maybe I just wish he was better,
at sending down some rope
when he gets so high
up the ladder that
I can barely
see him.

Would You Rather

"Let's play a game. Everyone all together."

Brad was a big guy.
Big enough that his suggestions were never really suggestions.
Big enough that his magnetism was more a matter
of physics than chemistry.

So we played a game. All together.
Sarah suggested "Would You Rather?"
and some of the boys rolled their eyes, pretending
they weren't happy to do literally anything
Sarah wanted to do.

Geoff nodded to Emily, Sammy, and me to come sit by him.
Or did he just nod to Emily?

Either way — the sophomores joined the senior circle.
The game was pretty easy to figure out.

"Would you rather have tongues for toes or toes for teeth?"
"Would you rather see through walls or see the future?"
"Would you rather bone a bone or screw a screw?"
Each time someone answered a question,
it was their turn to ask one.
The later the night got, the lewder the questions.

Until it was Emily's turn,
and she turned to me and asked,
"Omid — would you rather
be a river, or a lake,
or an ocean?"

And Then I Did Something Stupid

Something so so so so stupid.
I told her the truth.

"Ocean."

"Really? Why?"

I forgot where I was, who I was,
why I was there. All I saw, all I remembered
was Emily.

We were together, and it was getting late,
and she was looking into my eyes,
and she wanted to know more
about me.

It was all I ever wanted.
Why not tell her
everything?

"Because I'm most afraid of the ocean.
But if I *was* the ocean, that means
I'd probably be less afraid of it . . .
I think. Right?"

But it wasn't just us.
We were at a party.
At Geoff Sterling's house.
With the senior boys.

And the senior boys seriously suck.

SENIOR BOY #1: "What the hell kind of answer is that?"

SENIOR BOY #2: "Holy shit! What a fuckin' baby."

SENIOR BOY #3: "You're afraid of the ocean?"

SENIOR BOY #4: "Who's afraid of the ocean?"

SENIOR BOY #2: "I've heard of people being afraid of sharks, but — "

SENIOR BOY #1: "The ocean isn't coming for you, dude."

SENIOR BOY #4: "I mean, what do you expect from a desert dweller?"

Desert Dwellers

At first I didn't get it.
Because, at first, it felt normal.
It felt obvious and duh and shared. We were all
living in the desert. So we were all
desert dwellers, right?

Not quite.

Their laughs were growing louder,
drawing lines in the sand,
and learning how
to choose sides.

Their laughs were making it more
about the *kind* of desert one
dwelled in —

or was from.

The kind with cacti,
or the kind with camels?
The kind filled with friends,
or the kind filled with family?
Where the Tomahawks are made,
or where the Tomahawks are dropped?

I was a desert dweller afraid of water.
I was drying up, and Sammy
was there too,
laughing.

Have You Ever Wanted To Disappear?

I have. I did. Right then.

I wanted to enter a void. Or even better, become one.
Let me be a black hole forever. I wanted to be
anywhere but there.

Why did I say that?
What is wrong with me?
I'm a mistake made of
all the wrong words.

Lake! I should have said lake!

Emily's family has a lake house
somewhere far from here.
In some state that starts with *M*.
Minnesota? Michigan? Maine?
Maybe. It's somewhere beautiful
she goes to live in the summertime.

I want to go there, too.

And if I had just said lake,
maybe she would have invited me
to go there with her this summer.
And we could be a lake, together.
In a lake together.

We could swim, then lie on the dock.
My head in her lap. Her fingers in my hair.

I'd learn how to grill steaks with her dad.
I'd play board games with her mom.

And we would all laugh, together.

And the laughter would be
warm and soft. Like the sun setting.
Not cold or sharp, like the snickering
slicing through Geoff's room as
I held my breath and tried
to stop my heart
from beating.

Wild

A bottle appears
like a Pokémon in tall grass.
In the wild. The label reads
Dr. McGillicuddy's Fireball Cinnamon Whisky.
It's passed around. Sammy and Emily both
take a drink. I've been embarrassed
one too many times tonight to do anything else
that might attract more unwanted attention.

I can do this. I can play with fire too.

The drink tastes like Dr. McGillicuddy
tried to candy-coat rat poison.

I wonder if I'm going to die.

The room expands,
bigger somehow now
than it's ever been before.

Feeling deeply tired
in my body
and dizzy
in my head —
I just want to close my eyes,
for a little while.

I just want
to find a place
to rest.

Horizontal

I wake up in the wrong wing.

East Wing, I think? I seriously need a map.
I wake up on a couch at Geoff's house
out of place and have to pee.

It must be early,
because everyone is still asleep.
I dare not tread into the unknown,
into potential parental territory,
so I stand and stumble to safety,
sneaking slowly toward the bathroom
I saw in Geoff's room last night.

Sammy is sleeping on the floor.
I step over his arm as I realize
I don't remember falling asleep.
I wonder, for a second, what happened
here? What happens when I'm not around?

I start to recognize familiar landmarks in this foreign land.

The molding on the ceiling,
the artwork on the walls, even the rugs on the floor,
lead me back to where I was, last night.
The hallway to Geoff's room is littered
with swimsuits and disposable dinnerware.

There's so much room in this place for things to go unnoticed.
I wonder how many things are lost
in a house this big.

The party must have cleared out to wherever I was,
because Geoff's room is nearly empty.

Geoff is still here, asleep on his bed.
And Emily. Emily is here too.
On the bed. With Geoff.

I don't know what I'm seeing.
I don't want to know what I'm seeing.

My knees are trying to buckle,
but my stomach won't allow it.

They've both got their clothes on
and aren't even under the covers.

I'm overreacting.
Am I overreacting?

My brain starts looking for a way
to disprove the story
my eyes are telling.

"It's no big deal, Omid. You see them together
at school every day!" my brain exclaims,
desperate to believe.

"But not like this,"
my eyes reply.

"Not horizontal."

My Kingdom

Get to the bathroom.
Lock the door. Sit on the toilet like it's a throne,
and I'm a king and not some dumb kid. I'll stay in my kingdom.
Until I hear signs of life outside. Intelligent life.
Then I'll leave. Like I just woke up.
Like there's nothing to worry about!
Like everything will be just fine!
Like everything will be alright!
Like oh hey Emily oh hey Geoff didn't see you there!
Like great party last night, right? Totally. Had a blast.

I Escape

Out the sliding door and into the courtyard.
Out the courtyard and onto the driveway.
Down the winding road and through the neighborhood,
until the world is a desert wash,
until I am in the wilderness.

Until I am — somehow — on another hike.
This time, alone.

Home is out of sight
but close enough
to walk to. So I do.

I'm still afraid of yellow jackets,
of mountain lions, of being out here,
but I remember what Baba Joon said.

"This desert does not know who you are.
It has no expectations of you . . .
In nature you can be
whoever you want to be."

I take one step forward, then another,
sweating now but not bothered.

Actually, I'm kind of relieved.
Because nothing out here
has managed to kill me yet.

This is my desert.
Watch me dwell in it.

Coming Home

never felt so good.
I missed my room. I missed my bed.
I just want to brush my teeth.
And shower.
Get clean.
Get sleep.

But Amir looks up from the couch
as I try to sneak my way to the stairs.
"Yo!"

He's in the living room,
half watching TV, half taking off his shin guards.
Mom is there too, sitting at the dinner table
with three women I don't know.

"*Azizam!* I didn't know you were home.
When did you get here?"
"Oh, just now.
Sammy's mom dropped me off,
but she had to run."

"Well, make sure you invite her in next time!"
She turns to the ladies to say,
"We can probably convince Sharon to write a nice check."
Then she turns back to me.
"Omid, this is Beth, Laura, and Maya. They have kids at Nova
and are helping me organize a gala for your school next week."
"Nice to meet you,"
I say quickly, and make my way upstairs,
before I have to make anything else up.

Brothers, Part 2

"Why'd you lie?"
Amir is standing in my doorway.
What does he mean? What does he know?
"Huh? Lie about what?"
"Scott's dad drove us home from morning practice,
and I saw you. Walking on the side of the road by yourself."

I'm too tired to lie again.
"I don't want to talk about it."
"What's going on with you, bro?"
"I said I don't want to talk about it.
Now will you get out of here so I can shower?"
But Amir doesn't leave. He just stands there.
And then his face softens like we're playing chess,
and he's run out of moves.

And then, all of a sudden, I do want to talk about it.
"I went to Geoff's house last night. With Sammy. And Emily."
"You went where? Who's Geoff?"
"He's a senior. In the play with me. He was throwing a party."
"Who's Emily?"
"She's the new girl in my English class. Gave me that CD."
"Oh, right. Okay. And Sammy was with you?"
"Barely."
"What happened?"
"What you would expect, I guess. It was like a scene
from a bad movie. And I was stuck in it.
We played party games. People drank.
There were drugs too, I think."
Amir tilts his head. I know what he wants to ask,
and I know I don't want to tell him.

So, instead, I just say,
"Yeah, it was all really stupid."

"So . . . how'd you end up on the road?"
"People stayed the night. I fell asleep early on a couch.
Woke up this morning to go to the bathroom
and saw Emily sleeping next to Geoff.
I didn't want to be there anymore."

I stop talking because I've run out of moves, too.
Amir and I have never really talked like this.
I think I know what has to happen next,
but I don't know how to say it.
So Amir does it for me.

"Do you like Emily?"
I nod.

"That sucks. I'm sorry, man."

I look up at Amir. I want to say something
that will make it all not true. How I feel. What I saw.
Something that can make it all go away . . .
but I just don't have the magic words.

"How about you take a shower and then we play some *FIFA*?
You've been through a lot, so I might even
let you win."

And for the first time today, I laugh out loud.
"That sounds great."

A Rock Flies

through the air,
into the window at my dad's store,
and it's broken, again.

It's been happening a lot, lately.
A large glass wall made into a thousand sharp shards,
something beautiful
made dangerous,
overnight.

An alarm goes off.
It calls my dad's cell phone.
He wakes up and goes to work
at 3 a.m. to fix it.

In the morning,
he comes home,
and I ask him
if he's okay.

"Windows get broken.
It's normal, *baba*.
We must fix them
when they break."

I can't bring myself to tell him.
That I don't think that's normal.
That I don't want to fix them.
That I don't see why
we're the only ones
who have to.

Dad Goes Back To Bed

but I don't. I can't. I walk around
the house for what feels like an hour,
until my indignation dissipates
into something like annoyance,
which, over even more time,
finally gives way
to boredom.

Being bored is a special kind of sad.
Like a low-grade diet-soda sadness.

I haven't been bored in a bit.
And yet, here it is. I am overcome with the feeling
of being full — of nothing. It's unexpected. It's unwanted.

But being bored doesn't care if it's wanted.
It just shows up and hits you till you're down,
harder and harder until you finally get up
and do something, anything, about it.

Amir and I played *FIFA* all day yesterday.
That was fun. Could we play some more today?
No, he's got homework, and I should let him do it.
Maybe I should study my lines for the play?
We need to be off-book by Halloween.
But that's still two weeks away.

I've got plenty of time.
So much time until then.
Too much time until then.

I could listen to Emily's CD again.
But for the first time in a long time,
I don't want to think about Emily.

I wonder what happened.
I wonder when people left Geoff's house.
I wonder who was the last to leave.
I wonder if Sammy got home okay.
I wonder what to say to Sammy.

Oh shit.

I should probably listen to his CD.

Sammy's CD, Part 2

Holy. Freakin. Moly. Every. Single. Song. Is. Amazing.

Rewind. Repeat. Rewind. Repeat.
Rewind. Repeat. Rewind. Repeat.
Rewind. Repeat. Rewind. Repeat.
Rewind. Repeat. Rewind. Repeat.
Rewind. Repeat. Rewind. Repeat.
Rewind. Repeat. Rewind. Repeat.
Rewind. Repeat. Rewind. Repeat.
Rewind. Repeat. Rewind. Repeat.
Rewind. Repeat. Rewind. Repeat.
Rewind. Repeat. Rewind. Repeat.
Rewind. Repeat. Rewind. Repeat.
Rewind. Repeat. Rewind. Repeat.
Rewind. Repeat. Rewind. Repeat.
Rewind. Repeat. Rewind. Repeat.
Rewind. Repeat. Rewind. Repeat.
Rewind. Repeat. Rewind. Repeat.
Rewind. Repeat. Rewind. Repeat.
Rewind. Repeat. Rewind. Repeat.
Rewind. Repeat. Rewind. Repeat.
Rewind. Repeat. Rewind. Repeat.
Rewind. Repeat. Rewind. Repeat.
Rewind. Repeat. Rewind. Repeat.
Rewind. Repeat. Rewind. Repeat.
Rewind. Repeat. Rewind. Repeat.
Rewind. Repeat. Rewind. Repeat.
Rewind. Repeat. Rewind. Repeat.
Rewind. Repeat. Rewind. Repeat.
Rewind. Repeat. Rewind. Repeat.
Rewind. Repeat. Rewind. Repeat.
Rewind. Repeat. Rewind. Repeat.

This Music, Rap Music, Is Different

This music
is my whole
body tingling
whoa.
This music
is a current,
a flame, and
a flow.
This music
is a drive.
This music
is alive.
This music
doesn't hold back or worry
about feelings being spared.
This music
is not scared.
This music
is the right word
in the right place
at the right time.
Each rapper
takes the hardest
parts of life and
makes them
rhyme.
It's effortless
expression.

This music is perfection.

Live From Somewhere

On the very first track of Sammy's CD,
you hear a man speaking into a microphone
in front of a crowd. He greets the audience,

"Hellooooo, everybody! Recording live from somewhere . . ."

and then he passes the mic
to two rappers who ask the lord
for mercy, and start to tell a story.

It's their story.

The band is called Black Star,
and they fit so many words
into such a small amount of time
that I hear something new in each listen.
They throw out thoughts on Brooklyn and the Bible and
Bethlehem and Buddha and bullets and battling . . .
I'm not sure I could ever catch it all,
or ever understand it all,
but I want to.

They're talking about Brooklyn the whole time —
but that's just the setting for *this* story, for *their* story.

The more I listen, the more I think
the reason that man greeted us
and said they were recording
"live from somewhere"
is because it could be
live from anywhere.

Whole Worlds

It's been a few days,
and I won't stop (can't stop)
listening to Sammy's CD.

Sixteen tracks and I feel like I've downloaded
sixteen whole worlds into my head. Like each song
is a JPEG, and my brain is a modem,
and each listen is a pass where the image
comes into focus on the screen
just a little clearer.

Except these images are super high-res,
so it takes forever to see the whole picture,
and even when you think it's done loading,
it just keeps going,
it just keeps getting sharper.

And then,
there's the feeling.

That magic feeling.
That whole-body-tingling feeling.
That feeling of rolling down the windows
and blasting Persian music with Mom and Dad
and that feeling of being Bottom, of speaking in meter,
of performing Shakespeare's words, that feeling too.
It's all there.

On these sixteen tracks.

They're Talking About Iran

Dad and Baba Joon are in the living room
talking about the revolution.

They're considering the things they saw coming
and the things they didn't.

1979 feels like ancient history to me.
Or maybe more like a myth.

It's hard to believe
they were both there.

Mom and Maman Joon are in the kitchen
making *ghormeh sabzi* together
and playing Persian music.

I wander over to find them singing along
to some song I can't quite understand.
They don't see me. They start dancing.
For nobody but each other.

Mehmoonis with the whole family
happen less often than they used to.
The family from far away have all gone
back to their lives in other cities,
so we invite my grandparents
over to our house for dinner
more often.

While we eat, I notice
there's something missing

from the way we talk
with my grandparents.

We don't tell them everything.

(And it has nothing to do with a language barrier,
because Mom and Dad do it too.)

Dad doesn't disclose the store window being broken,
just like Mom never mentioned the man in the parking lot.
We mostly talk about easy stuff, and eat way too much food,
and try to catch up on a few decades
of not sitting in the same room.

When it's time for our post-dinner show-and-tell,
I start to wonder . . .

What if that man from the top of Sammy's CD

          was here,
                right now,
                         with my family?

What if he'd brought his microphone?

    ("Hellooooo, everybody! Recording live from Tucson . . .")

What if he passed it around?

What if we actually talked
about *our* hard stuff . . .
our broken windows,
our broken smiles,

201

our broken English,
our broken Farsi,
our broken bonds
from being apart
from each other for so long
that we don't really know
how to be together?

Could we make that rhyme?

I think about Mom rapping. Dad rapping.
Baba Joon and Maman Joon too.

What would they say?

But the man from Sammy's CD isn't here.
There's no microphone being passed around.
And even if there were, Dad probably wouldn't trust it.

So I guess we're stuck with the usual.

Maman Joon goes first.
She brings out her big book of Persian poetry.
She reads a poem by Hafez, then one by Rumi,
then looks at my mom and smiles. I don't know why.
When it's Baba Joon's turn, he starts to tell a joke in Farsi,
then switches to English halfway through.
The punch line gets lost in translation. My dad half laughs
as he passes around a full-page ad for his store in the paper.

Then my parents ask if Amir and I want to share something,
    and I start to feel   that feeling   in my chest again
                                            and I start to spiral

because there's nothing I can do.
                          Nothing I can contribute. They ask me
             to perform a Shakespeare monologue from the show—
                          but it's not ready yet. I'm not
                                  ready yet. I want them to see me
                                        when I'm perfect.

Amir speaks up.

He offers to do some freestyle tricks,
and everyone follows him into the backyard
to watch him juggle his soccer ball like a hundred times,
then balance it on his foot, then on his knee,
then on his head, then on his foot again,
and then everyone cheers,
because everyone
is happy.

Taking Attendance

Mr. Thompson isn't at school today,
so we have a substitute teacher
running our rehearsal.

"Hate" is a strong word.
I only hate like five things.

Substitute teachers
taking attendance
is one of them.

A Question I Must Answer

Every time they take attendance,
"Omid" becomes a speed bump,
a proceed with caution,
or even a stop sign.

But "Geoff" is full speed
and blue skies ahead.
His phonetic obstacles
are hurdled with ease.

"G-E-O-F-F" becomes "Jeff,"
a normal word,
a normal person,
instantly.

But Omid gets butchered, shortened, or stretched.
It becomes an "ohm" or an "ummm?"
My name becomes a question I must answer.

"It's O-mee-d."

"Ohh! That's a pretty name. Where are you from?"

"My parents are from Iran," I always say,
knowing that saying, "I'm from Tucson"
will only lead to another question.

But "Geoff" becomes Jeff.
A person, not a question.

Geoff answers to no one.

Crown

The substitute tells me to report
to the costume shop for my fitting.

I tell her I didn't know
we had a costume shop, and I don't know where it is.
Our stage manager agrees to walk me over.
She takes me out behind the theater,
and I see it.

"Costume shop" is . . . generous.

It's a muggy mobile home with no air-conditioning,
filled with trunks, bins, and racks of donated clothes
from what looks like every decade of Nova's existence.

I've never met the woman who's working in here,
but she seems to be expecting me.

"You must be Omid."
She mispronounces my name too.
"And you're playing Bottom, is that right?"
"Uh, yes, ma'am."

She smiles, then disappears
behind one of the hundred costume racks.
"Alright, so you're our donkey . . ."
She's talking about the top of act three.

"You ready for your crown, darlin'?"
she says as she reappears,
stepping through a curtain of clothing,

holding a small box and a pair of
long, floppy, moth-eaten
donkey ears.

I take the ears.
I put them on my head.

Then she opens the small box and my stomach turns.
It's a set of comically large, overly ugly teeth.

I don't know what to do.

"Oh, don't you worry, they're clean. Washed 'em myself.
Now just pop those in and smile so I can take a quick picture."

I reach for the teeth. I put them in my mouth.
I turn around and look in the mirror.
And for a split second,
I don't recognize myself.

I remember rehearsing the top of act three.
I remember Rebecca yelling, "Thou art translated!"
I feel nauseous. I don't know how it happened.
How I got here. Alone. Looking
in the mirror — at a literal jackass.
Transformed. Half horror, half humor.
Like the punch line of Baba Joon's joke.
Lost in translation.

Flow

I sneak back into the theater,
and sit in the back row,
and pull out my Walkman,
and put on my headphones,
and press play on Sammy's CD.

I let each lyric wash over me.

I make myself invisible
for the rest of rehearsal.
I don't want to be seen.
I don't want to see
anybody . . . Emily
especially.

I don't know how
to ask her, or even *if*
I should ask her, about
what I saw at Geoff's.

I call Sammy as soon as I get home.

I ask him about Black Star
and A Tribe Called Quest and Outkast.
I want to know more about rap. I want to go beyond
the band names.

He tells me Outkast is Big Boi and Andre 3000.
He tells me Black Star is Mos Def and Talib Kweli.
He tells me A Tribe Called Quest is Q-Tip and Phife Dawg.

I try to imagine each of their faces
like I imagine the faces of relatives
on the other end of the line
when my parents call Iran.
I feel like Sammy and I
are getting closer
to something important.

I tell him my favorite moments on his mix
are when one rapper calls
and another rapper answers, in time and in tune.
The bands all do it.
Eminem does it with Jay-Z.
Nas does it with Puff Daddy.
As if to say, "I hear you, and I'm here too."
As if to help, to continue carrying the thought,
taking it places the other couldn't go.
Sammy calls it "complementary flow."
There's that word again!

Flow.

It came to my mind the first time I listened to Sammy's CD.
I think that word, that feeling, is the key to understanding why
I like what I'm hearing.

"So — what exactly do you mean when you say 'flow'?"

Sammy laughs.

"You're a real noob, dude . . . Every rapper has their own way
of riding a beat, phrasing their bars, slanting their rhymes . . .
That's their flow."

I don't know why I'm so surprised
to hear how much Sammy knows about this stuff.
I've always gone to him for secret access to cool guy knowledge.
But this is different. Maybe I'm surprised —
because he sounds so excited
to be sharing it
with me.

He goes on,

"It can take years to find
your flow. But once you do,
it's like tapping into
a superhero state."

Then Sammy Asks Me Something

I should have seen coming,
something I probably should have
had an answer for
but didn't . . .

"Yo dude — by the way — what happened to you on Saturday?
I woke up and you were just gone."
"Oh yeah. Umm . . .
I felt pretty sick in the morning.
And I didn't wanna bother you or anyone.
So I left."

"You just left? Like — how?"
"Yeah. I walked home.
Geoff's place isn't too far from my house."

"Damn. Alright.
So you felt super sick — but you walked all the way home?"
"Yep," I say, and immediately start scanning my story
for any other obvious plot holes
I'll have to fill on the fly.

"Well, listen —
I just wanted to say
I'm sorry about Friday
and not having your back
when I should have."

"What? No, dude. It's all good.
I mean, what do you even mean?"

"I feel like some shit was being said
that I didn't really agree with, and I was
laughing along at some jokes that weren't really
funny. I dunno. Just wanted to say my bad, is all."

Desert dweller.

I know immediately that's what he means.
I know he knows it hurt me, but I thought
it was something we'd just file away
under "forget about it."

Sammy keeps finding new ways to surprise me.

"Thanks," I say.

He goes quiet.
I think about telling him more.
Telling him the truth. Like I told Amir.
I think about telling him why I left.
How I found Emily and Geoff.

But I don't.
Because telling Sammy will make it
even more real than telling Amir did.
Which doesn't make sense,
but I know it the same way
I know gravity exists.

So instead I leave it at,
"Thanks, dude. We're good."

Powerful

On the chorus of "Renegade,"
Jay-Z and Eminem
sing together.

They sing about how they've never been afraid
to speak up. To tell people
what they're thinking.
About anything.

Anything.

I mean, how is that even possible?
To have *never* been afraid?
How can someone speak up,
speak out about a thing
they know might
make others
upset?

Flow (verb)
1. To run, to move, or change form like fluid
2. To come in like a tide, to rise

Flow (noun)
1. The act of flowing
2. A superhero state

When Jay-Z and Eminem exchange verses,
their words converge in theme
while somehow still carrying
very personal perspectives.

They remember what the world gave them
growing up and point out what it didn't.
They celebrate
how they persevered,
how they conquered it anyway.

Then, on his last verse, Eminem does this thing
that absolutely blows my mind.

He flows
above the beat
and under it
and through it.
He writes these lines,
rhymes that feel
inevitable.

He compares himself to Shakespeare.

To the very greatest
that ever was.
And he's so confident,
he's so good at rapping,
you find yourself
believing him.

And that's when he chooses to tear it all down.

The whole idea of heroes
and villains. He points out
how people always project
their own tastes and standards,

how they will always be looking
for the next best
and the next worst
thing.

I love it.
And I can almost do it.
I can almost rap that whole verse with him.
It's about getting your tongue to move faster than it thinks
it can because once your tongue knows what comes next
you can actually just turn off your brain and repeat it
over and over until it becomes muscle memory.
And that's when it starts
to feel powerful.

Powerful, Part 2

In seventh-grade bio we learned that the tongue
is the strongest muscle in the whole human body.

Something about its proportional power.

I thought that was pretty weird.

I remember imagining a tongue
trying to kick a soccer ball, which was
(a) very gross and (b) ineffective.

But now I'm starting to think about it another way.

Maybe the strength of the tongue isn't about kicking a ball.
Maybe the tongue is especially strong
when it does what only it can do.
When it molds thought into sound,
when it makes words.

The Joke Of The Scene

Mr. Thompson is back at rehearsal.

We finished staging the end of the show,
and now we're starting from the top.

Which means we're about to hit my first scene again,
where Bottom is being cast in the play
and wants to play every character,
and the joke of the scene is
how badly he wants it.

I thought it was going well,
but after a few runs,
Mr. Thompson asks me
to join him in the audience.

When I do, he says something I don't expect.

"Alright, Omid—I know you've got more in you.
I want you to make bolder choices.
I want you to go back up there and try
to really surprise your castmates
in this next run. The bigger the better."

I thought I was already being big, but apparently not,
because Mr. Thompson wants more.
I don't have any idea how to be
"bigger," and I feel more confused
than creative, so maybe
I can just pull something
from real life for now?

Bottom is superconfident.
Who do I know in my life
who's superconfident?

Sammy, for sure.
And Amir. And Dad.

But Bottom is loud, too.
And Sammy and Amir don't get super loud super often.
While Dad, on the other hand . . .

I go onstage to do the scene again,
but this time when Bottom is about to pretend
to be a tyrant, I drop the octave of my voice
and elongate all my *a*'s and turn all my *w*'s into *v*'s
and make my voice sound
like my dad's.

And to my surprise — it works.

Everyone is laughing
harder than they ever have before.
I look over to Mr. Thompson in the audience
as he uncrosses his arms, smiles,
and gives me two big thumbs-up.

A Second Too Long

"That was ridiculous!"

I turn around and see
Emily, standing there
smiling, so pretty
it hurts.

"Oh — "

"Like seriously, so funny,
so good, Omid."

"Thanks, Em."

I look at her
for a second too long.
It gets awkward.
I start to say,

"So hey — "

But she cuts me off.

"Sorry, I gotta get going.
Lots of homework tonight . . .
But I'll see you tomorrow."

"Totally, totally . . . See ya soon."

Back Home In Bed

Something feels off.
                        About the day.
                        About the play.

Like rehearsal wasn't right,
but I don't quite
know why.

It could just be me
overthinking again.

                                I load up Sammy's CD,
                                put on my headphones,
                                and press play.

(I See No) Changes

Mos Def and Talib Kweli sing for Tupac and Biggie,
like Baba Joon sings for his sister.

All of them
    singing songs
that rhyme
    with prayer.

At The Grocery Store, Again

This time with Baba Joon.

We broke off from the family mid-*mehmooni*
and went on what felt like a field trip.
He'd said he wanted to make a treat, something sweet,
but needed to get ingredients from the store.

That sounded good to me.

So I offered to come,
thinking I could help him
with his grocery list.

When we got here,
I just started pointing at things,
naming them in Farsi,
and he didn't even have to ask me,
cuz this is how you *tarof*
in the dairy aisle.

        (Right?)

  "Paneer!"

                   "Khameh!"

        "Kareh!"

                      "Mahst!"

Baba Joon reaches for a carton of milk —
but before I can say, *"Sheer!"*
he looks at me and says, in English, "Milk!"
then turns away and plows toward the produce
like he's had enough schooling for the day.

Okay.
It's probably for the best we stop.
I mean, I was running out of words anyway.
But I don't get it — did I do something wrong?

The man is on a mission,
and as he's reaching his next objective
(some bananas), I notice Baba Joon's red polo shirt
stretching over his belly, awkwardly,
like my shirts sometimes do.

I find myself getting frustrated.

Thinking how, if it were me, I would sneak away
into an aisle where no one could see me
to stuff my arms deep down my sleeves
and stretch the whole midsection of the shirt out
till no one could see it sticking
to my stomach.

But he doesn't even notice.
Or, maybe, he doesn't even care?

Simple, Like Sheermoz

Back at the house, Baba Joon and I
are huddled over the blender in the kitchen.

"Put three or four bananas in the blender.
Pour enough milk to cover them all up.
Add a little bit of honey, extra if you've had a bad day.
Then blend,"

he says as he flips a switch,
and the kitchen is flooded
with the roar of blender blades
mincing anything in their path,
melting everything into liquid.

I'm startled by the sound.
I take a few steps back
and go to cover my ears.

Baba Joon laughs
and says something
I can't hear over the chaos
as he shrugs his shoulders
with his hands out to his sides, palms up open,
squinting his eyes, as if to say, "C'mon, it's not that bad,"
then makes his hands into fists, frowns, and flexes his arms,
as if to add, "We are mighty men making milkshakes!"

I take my hands off my ears.
I flex too. I laugh
with him.

Baba Joon turns off the blender and pours two glasses.
He puts one in front of me and says,

"Sheermoz. My favorite drink,
ever since I was your age."

He takes a sip — then reaches for the honey and pours more in.

"Had a bad day?" I smile.

"When you get old, Omid jan,
people will think
you cannot see anymore,
you cannot hear anymore,
that you cannot tell
what is happening in the world anymore,
that you do not know the difference
between being loved
and being respected,
but I have ears,
I have eyes,
I still have a mind,
no matter what
anyone wishes."

He looks outside, where everyone else is,
my mom, my dad, my grandma, and Amir.

"They think I am simple, like sheermoz."

He takes another sip,
licks his lips, and goes on.

"A little milk, a little banana.
And sometimes honey, for the hard days.
Simple. But me? No. Please. I never was —
never will be — "

He stops.

And I realize — this is it.
This is what I've been waiting for.
Something is changing — between us —
something real is being said, and it didn't take
some supersmart talk about Shakespeare —
just a trip to the grocery store —
just a bit of time.

I choose my next words
as carefully as I can.

"So then — then what are you, Baba Joon?"

Notice

He takes his time to answer.
So much time, in fact, I start to think

he might actually know.

He might actually be about to show me
how to tell someone else
exactly who you are.

He looks at me,
and his eyes grow full,
so full they become heavy,
so heavy they start to close.

And that's when I know,
whatever he was going to say
is gone. And it isn't coming back.

"I'm tired."

He exhales.

"And old.
Or at least older than I was
when I thought I could ever know
the answer to that question.
Older than you.

You have so much time left, Omid.
You must begin to notice
how people see you.

And how they are going to
see you, now that those planes
have gone into those buildings,
have changed this place."

He rubs his temples as he speaks,
like he's remembering the past,
like he's predicting the future.

"One day it's one way,
and the next it's not,
and I just want
you to know —

They will blame.
They will blame me.
They will blame you.
They will blame everyone
but themselves."

He opens his eyes.

"They will make a mess.
And you must notice. All of it.
But do not become a part of it.

Because this way of seeing people
as other people, as different from one another,
it helps no one but those who are looking for simple answers.

And we are not simple.
Not me, not you, not them.
None of us."

I'm realizing I haven't been breathing.

I'm realizing he didn't know
he would be saying any of this to me,
not a few months ago, not a few minutes ago.

I'm realizing this is the first time
anyone's talked to me about 9/11 like this.

I'm realizing how often people
at school, or at home, just stop talking,
or change the subject when I walk into the room.

I'm realizing he's talking to me
like I'm an adult. And I am so
grateful for it.
For him.

"Merci, Baba Joon."

"Merci, Baba Joon"

It's all I can say.
But not all I want to say.

It's moments like these,
where understanding Farsi
better than I'm able to speak it,
keeps me confined to the kids' table.
I was grateful.

But I was also — frustrated.
Because what Baba Joon just told me
was big. Big enough to ring both true and false,
and, as usual, I didn't have the words to tell him that.

Something in his speech felt right.

About the mess that's being made
and about the way they'll blame
people like him,
people like me.
But at the same time,
I know people *like* me.

So something in his speech felt wrong too.

I mean, my friends know — they must know — I'm different
from all those angry people who kind of look like me
yelling "Death to America" on TV. And I know,
if I needed to, I could prove it.

I'm different.

Halloween

I don't know how it happened.
How I managed to forget what day it was.
Everyone at school was wearing their costume.

Even Headmaster Frankel got into it,
roaming the school grounds as Frankelstein's Monster.
I usually dress up. Usually pick a character,
from a favorite movie or game,
and go for it.

But today, I forgot.
Today, I felt stranger in my everyday Omid clothes
than I would have in a costume.

I must have thought I had more time.

Because today was also the cast deadline
to be off-book for *Midsummer*.
And I totally missed it.

So I faked it for a bit.

I had a bunch of lines in my head, from past rehearsals,
and used my scene partners to help me guess which ones
fit the moment and which ones didn't. I tried to find
the right things to say and somehow got pretty far.

Until act four, scene one.
Until I had to do that stupid monologue
alone onstage with no one to turn to —
and I went blank. Not once. Not twice.

But   on   every   single   line.

And as my actual memory failed me,
my muscle memory wanted to kick in,
wanted to spit Eminem's "Renegade" verse,
faster than the speed of thought, just to prove
that I was worth something.

But I stopped my tongue
from saying one man's words
in place of another's.

Then I started to sweat.

I started to wonder if I was breathing
alright. I started to have a sneaking suspicion
that this might be about more than this rehearsal.
That this might be about everything and all of it.
Mr. Thompson started throwing me
prompts. He tried
to help.

But I couldn't hear him.

Repeat, After Me

AMIR
"When my cue comes, call me, and I will
answer: my next is, 'Most fair Pyramus.'"

OMID
"When my cue comes, call me, and I will
answer it: my next one is, 'Most fair Pyramus.'"

AMIR
Not quite. You added "it" after "answer" and "one" after "next."

I asked Amir to help me learn my lines.
I asked him to hold my feet to the fire
and make sure I was word-perfect.
I want to know these lines so well
that no one will remember me
not knowing them.

AMIR
"The eye of man hath not heard, the ear of man hath not
seen, man's hand is not able to taste, his tongue to conceive,
nor his heart to report, what my dream was."

OMID
"The eye of man hath not heard, the ear of man hath not
seen, man's hand is not able to taste, his tongue to conceive,
nor his heart to report, what my dream was."

AMIR
That was great. Good job, dude. But I don't really get it.

OMID

You don't get what?

AMIR

Like what he's saying. The senses are all mixed up.

OMID

Yeah, exactly, that's the whole idea. At this point in the play he's just woken up from a spell, so he's kinda groggy, and he's about to transition back to his normal life from this crazy forest fantasy. So he's confused. He knows what he saw, what he heard, what he felt, but he knows how crazy it will sound if he tells anyone the truth. On top of all that, Shakespeare is doing that thing where he keeps reminding the audience that Bottom is an ass, with or without the donkey's head. There's a lot going on.

AMIR

Ohhh — that actually makes the next bit make more sense. When he asks Quince to make his story a part of their play.

OMID

Exactly! You get it.

AMIR

Right. Okay, let's do that part. Ready?
"I will get Peter Quince to write a ballad of
this dream: it shall be called Bottom's Dream,
because it hath no bottom."

OMID

"I will get Quince to write me a ballad of
this dream and it shall be called Bottom's Dream,
because it has no bottom."

AMIR

Almost, but nope. Listen a little closer.
"I will get Peter Quince to write a ballad of
this dream: it shall be called Bottom's Dream,
because it hath no bottom."

OMID

"I will get Peter Quince to write a ballad of
this dream: it shall be called Bottom's Dream,
because it hath no bottom."

AMIR

There you go. Perfect. You know, this is kind of funny. It's like we
switched parts.

OMID

Which parts?

AMIR

I mean, I'm usually the one repeating after you — like repeating
everything you've already done.

He pauses. Then goes on.

AMIR

It's like I'm stuck. In your past, in an echo of all the things you've
done, and sometimes I don't want to know what's coming? Does
that make sense?

OMID

I — no — I mean — what have I even done? Compared to you,
I'm — pretty unimpressive. I've never had a girlfriend. I've never
been the captain of any team. I can barely even run a lap.

235

AMIR

Are you kidding? Every time we get an assignment in class, your project just happens to be the one the teachers use as an "outstanding creative interpretation from a past student." Ms. Martin won't shut up about your *Julius Caesar* project.

OMID

Umm. I filled a vase with G.I. Joes.

AMIR

Yeah, I know. "Our legions are brim-full." Brutus, act four, scene three.

OMID

So what?

AMIR

So, I saw you spend fifteen minutes on it — and you got an A. It takes most people hours to do anything "A" worthy at Nova.

Another moment passes.

OMID

We should get back to work.

AMIR

Work?

OMID

The scene. There's only a few lines left. Let's finish it.

AMIR

Oh, right, sure. But this doesn't really feel like work to me.

I smile because he's right, it doesn't. He smiles too.

AMIR
I mean, this is actually kinda fun.

OMID
Yeah, it is.

The Clock Strikes Midnight

NIGHT.

Upstairs: AMIR is asleep. OMID is word-perfect
on his Shakespeare and back to listening to SAMMY's CD.

Downstairs: MOM and DAD enter the house.
They are coming home from a ball.
OMID takes off his headphones when he feels
the garage door open. His parents are arguing in Farsi.
He can hear every word.

DAD
Are you okay?

MOM
Oh, so he is alive.

DAD
What is that supposed to mean?

MOM
Nothing. It means nothing. Glad you haven't forgotten how to
speak.

DAD
Ten thousand dollars for your charity, and still, I've done
something wrong?

MOM
My charity?! That donation was for the kids' school.

DAD

I thought the tuition paid for the kids' school. But no, nothing is ever good enough for you.

MOM

Good enough for me? What's good enough for you? Are these friends of yours good enough for you?

DAD

What the hell are you talking about?

MOM

Let Bob say whatever he wants when it's just the two of you, but please, not in front of me. Have enough dignity not to let him talk that way around me.

DAD

Talk what way?

MOM

For God's sake, you're Muslim! Not me! This should offend you! Not me! How can you just stand there as he fouls the air with his hate?

DAD

Oh, that's what this is about?

He laughs.

Don't let that ruin your mood, sweetheart. Bob doesn't know what he's saying.

MOM

But he does know what he's saying. And you know that none of it is true. You lived in Iran, remember?

DAD

So now it's my responsibility to change Bob? Please, don't waste my time.

MOM

Waste your time? This is a waste of time to you?

DAD

No. Trying to change Bob is a waste of time. Who cares what Bob thinks?

MOM

You're Muslim!

DAD

Yes, I'm Muslim! But I don't go shouting my religion from the rooftops like your family.

MOM

That's different.

DAD

No, it's not. That's what your family chooses to do, this is what I choose to do. I don't care what Bob believes. Bob doesn't care what I believe. And it's just words. Stupid words. It means nothing.

MOM

It starts with words. Then it becomes actions. How do I know what he might do one day? To you? To me?

DAD

If Bob ever touches you, I'll kill him myself.

MOM

Don't say that!

DAD

Then stop overreacting! What am I supposed to do? Without
Bob and his friends — do you think we would be living here?
Do you think Omid and Amir would be going to private schools?

MOM

What the fuck does that mean? We don't owe anything to those
assholes. We bought this house. We pay the tuition. I am the chair
of their charity!

DAD

But where does all the money come from?! My friends — and
my friends' friends — buy the rugs! You want me to destroy
everything we've built because ignorant Bob has never left
Arizona?!

The clock strikes midnight.

MOM

Good night. You can sleep down here tonight.

DAD

Happily. And you're welcome! And congratulations on your
fucking ball!

The Weaver

I like to think of Bottom at home,
weaving. A rug. A tapestry.
A masterpiece
in process.

                                He is quiet when he's alone.

He thinks hard, considering each thread with care.
Which textures should be knotted together?
Which color complements the others?
This is his work.
To decide.

Nick Bottom is overwhelmed
                        by his loom.
                        He's afraid of what that might mean.

He can't wait to go to rehearsal
                        to play
with Quince and Snug,
and sure, Francis too.

He's never been in love,
                but he knows how it's supposed to look.
                        How it's supposed to feel.

The hero, the lover, the lion, the tyrant.
The weaver.
Bottom wants it all
                to fit together.

And when it actually does, with Titania,
for the briefest of moments . . . he acts real cool about it.
Like it's no big thing. Until the brief moment passes.

And then he convinces himself

it was all
            some kind
                        of dream.

Nick

But what really gets me, though,
why I really feel for Nick,
is that it kind of . . . was.

It was a dream.
No. It was worse.
It was a prank.

What did the poor guy do to deserve all that?

Yes, he's loud when others are quiet.
Yes, he uses words the wrong way sometimes.
Yes, he strives to rise above, to be special.

Maybe he just wants a better life.

Is that really reason enough
to point and laugh?

Is that really reason enough
to make him a monster?

Doogh

Dad doesn't come to our grandparents' house on Sunday.

When Mom, Amir, and I arrive, Baba Joon is watching
an Iranian news program on the TV,
and Maman Joon is in the kitchen
making something sweet to eat.

Baba Joon asks where my dad is,
and Mom begins to explain,
but doesn't make it
to the end of her sentence
before she starts to cry.

Maman Joon glares at Baba Joon.
He turns off the TV and stands up to hug Mom.
"It's okay. It's okay, darling. You can tell me what's wrong . . ."
he says as he leads her to their bedroom.

"Come here, boys."

Maman Joon calls us to the kitchen, where
there are pomegranates, walnuts, and dried mint leaves
on the counter, next to some cinnamon, sugar, and salt.

"Are you thirsty? I can make some doogh."
"Yes, please," I say immediately,
because who could say no to *doogh*?
We watch as she grinds dried mint with a pinch of salt
and sprinkles the mixture atop blended yogurt,
club soda, and ice water.

Then we hear a thud.

The three of us look up at the window, and Maman Joon sighs.
"Oh no. Every time your Baba Joon cleans this window,
another poor bird flies right into it. Amir, go get
me my broom and dustpan from the garage.
I'll move it before it brings out the coyotes."

"It's okay, Maman Joon!
You finish the doogh, I'll throw away the bird."

"You're a good boy, Amir.
Wash your hands when you're finished."
Amir runs toward the garage.

I want to offer to help too,
but I don't want to touch a dead bird.

As soon as Amir is outside,
Mom and Baba Joon return from the bedroom.
Neither seems happier than they were before.
Today's visit will be short.

Mom and Maman Joon head out to our car
to load the trunk with enough *fesenjoon*
to feed us for a week.
It's my dad's favorite dish.

I ask Baba Joon how he's doing.

"I'm excellent, Omid jan."

He asks me if the play is getting easier.

"It is."
A half lie.

"Are you still making your sheermoz with extra honey?
Or is America getting easier?"
I try to speak in longer sentences.
I want to be able to joke with him.
He smiles but doesn't laugh.

"Don't worry about me, Omid. I am okay."

Why did that sound
like another
half lie?

"And what about my mom? . . . Is she okay?"

"Yes. She is okay.

You know, this place can be hard for anyone.
No matter how long you've been here.
America is so young
its people don't know what to make of it yet.
Your mom and dad love each other very much.
But they love America for different reasons, Omid jan.

Your dad came to America to be rich.
Your mom came to America to be free."

The Same But Different

Mom and Dad came to America —
they love America —
for different reasons.

Why can't I stop thinking
about what Baba Joon said?

How two people can agree to do the same thing,
         without agreeing why they're doing it.

                How you might not ever even notice it,
                    if you are always satisfied with
                        what you see on the surface,
                            if you never look
                                a little deeper.

Now I'm thinking about rehearsal, about that funny feeling,
about Mr. Thompson, about Bottom, about
all of Shakespeare's words

in my mouth and how I'm saying them.

I'm wondering why
I wanted this
in the first place.

                                    I remember wanting
                        Baba Joon and Maman Joon to see me
                    in the play. But I wonder how much of me
                is left in there. I remember the audition with Emily.
                    How it felt so good. So right. But now I feel
                        so far away from all that.

Mr. Thompson wants Bottom more,
wants Bottom big. But big didn't feel good.
Even if it once did. It doesn't anymore.

                                        Something's changed.

Those laughs

didn't feel right.
Not to me. It's like people were seeing
something they wanted to see, but not
what I wanted them to see.

Not me.

It's a play, they'll say.
It's just pretend. But there needs to be
a way to play, even to pretend,
without being the butt
of the joke.

Is this why
I was put in this part?
To be laughed at?

No one is laughing at Emily.
No one is laughing at Geoff.

What did I agree to
when I agreed to
play Bottom?

Funny

Sarah keeps saying,
"It was funnier last time,"
or "I think we can make it funnier than that,"
or "No one is laughing at our scene anymore, Omid!"

Sarah is playing Titania,
and she thinks our scene
should be funny.

This is probably because
Sarah has never been in love
with someone who doesn't love her back.

The way I see it, Titania is under a spell.
Literally. She's completely obsessed with Bottom.
And I think that's probably new for Bottom. And I think
Bottom is pretty confused about it, to be honest.

I'm trying to be honest.
Trying to be Nick, Bottom, and Omid too.
But Sarah thinks I should be funny.

So she says, "Try that voice you did last time,
that was really funny! The super-deep
voice that sounded Russian or Arab
or something . . ."

My dad's voice.
"No.
                    I don't want to do that again."

Now she's getting frustrated.
Like our scene is failing
all because of me.

"Well, we have to try something, cuz this isn't working for me.
And Mr. Thompson obviously asked you
to change something last time too . . .
So just make another choice.
A big one."

I start to wonder
how many choices
I have left.

And that's when she says,
"Oh, I know! Let's try it another way.
Let's try Bottom falling totally
head over hooves in love
with Titania!
Maybe that would
be funny."

I don't think that's really
the right way to go,
so I start to say,

"I don't know — "

But Sarah is pissed by this point and snaps back,

"Sure you do.
Just pretend
I'm Emily."

Dramatic Irony

is when the whole audience knows something
that the main character doesn't.

Dramatic irony is what makes an ass out of Bottom.
Has dramatic irony made an ass out of me, too?

How did Sarah know?
How long has Sarah known?

Who else knows?
                        Oh no.
                                Is it that obvious?

                                        I think I'm gonna be sick.

So I Leave

I walk right out of rehearsal,
out of the theater,
out of that
mess.

I just need a breath
of fresh air.

I wait for Emily,
I pray for Emily,
to come out after me,
but she doesn't.

Instead, the stage door opens,
and it's Mr. Thompson who appears
looking angry, with Sarah behind him
trying to explain how none of this is her fault.

I duck behind some lockers
till they both give up looking.

I hide and stay hidden

until I see Mom's car driving toward parent pickup
and I run for it — faster than I've run for anything in my life —
almost as fast as Amir running toward a secret desert waterfall.

Do I Need To Remind You

Amir is already in the car,
and as soon as I get in,
Mom suggests we go visit
my grandparents.

It's not that I don't want to go.
I just wasn't expecting it,
you know?

Okay, so maybe I don't want to go.

But I'm pretty sure Amir feels the same way,
cuz he looks at me and crosses his eyes,
rolls them back into his head,
and sticks out his tongue
like he is dying
in a cartoon.

I hold in a laugh, but Mom sees it and isn't interested
in entertaining our brief fling with disrespect.

"Do I need to remind you both
that they moved across the entire planet,
that they left behind all their friends,
and everything they've ever known,
just so they could come live
closer to you two?"

No.

She did not have to remind us of that.

Back To Backgammon

We had only been at my grandparents' house for five minutes
when Mom turned to us to say,

*"Okay, boys, I have to take my mom to the Persian market.
You stay here with Baba Joon."*

And then, as if she knew exactly what we were both thinking,
added in English,

"Don't nag. We'll go home as soon as I get back."

Then switched back to Farsi,

*"Baba Joon wants to teach you
how to play backgammon!
You guys are so lucky. Because
Dad is one of the best players
in our whole family."*

Then she got into her car with Maman Joon,
and they drove away.

Amir and I sat across the board from each other,
trying not to look bored as Baba Joon explained the rules.
The game wasn't super intuitive,
so we just mirrored each other's moves.

Baba Joon explained
which section of the board was home, where you want to go,
and which section of the board was jail, where you don't.

He told us double sixes are the best roll,
because they give you the most mobility,
and warned us to never leave
a piece alone.

He put a single piece out on the board,
pointed to it, and said in English,
"Very bad, boys. I hit easy. You go jail."

That's when I laughed.

Not too loud. And honestly not at anything, really.
At first it was soft and stupid and harmless.
Until Amir heard it, picked it up, and ran with it.
Until he started laughing really hard.
Which made me laugh really hard too.

And it felt good.

To be laughing
in the middle
of everything.

To be on the inside,
looking out,
for once.

But Baba Joon wasn't inside.

He didn't know why we were laughing.
Which makes sense, because we barely knew why
we were laughing. It just — felt so good.
I think we just needed to feel good and let go.

For a bit. And I could tell he didn't get it,
or was getting uncomfortable, so I tried to explain.
"It's nothing, Baba Joon. I just started laughing
because I didn't understand the rules,
and then when Amir started laughing
it made me laugh even harder,"
but then I realized I was trying to explain this all in English,
which he didn't really speak, so I started waving my hands
to try to communicate that no really
this is no big deal, just give us a second to reset . . .
which made the whole thing even funnier. To the point
where Amir and I were both crying and trying
to avoid eye contact, scared that it would
set us off again.

Baba Joon didn't understand.

And for some reason,
he wouldn't, or couldn't,
just laugh along.
He must have thought
we were laughing
at him.

He must have.

Because that's when he stood up,
clenched his fists, and slammed them into the board,
sending all the pieces flying, then turned around,
kicked the door open,
and left the room.

Amir and I came down from our fit pretty quick after that.

"Holy shit. What was that about?"
"I don't know, dude."
"What do we do now?"
"No idea."

After a few minutes,
we crept out to the living room,
where Baba Joon was watching
a satellite-dish program on TV
in Farsi.

"Are you alright, Baba Joon?"
I asked.

But Baba Joon didn't answer.
He didn't say anything.
He wouldn't even
look at us.

Amir looked at me,
and I could tell he
was worried.

"Let's just go do our homework
in the other room until Mom gets back."

And that's exactly what we did.
All the while wondering if we should
try to figure out what just happened
or try harder to forget it.

The Iceberg

Dad sold the rug.

The small square silk one from Qom.
But I don't think he knew
that Maman Joon never told Baba Joon
that she asked Dad to sell it.

So when Dad went to give Baba Joon all that money,
Baba Joon didn't know what it was for.

Now, I don't quite get
why it was such a big deal,
but it was *such* a big deal.

Baba Joon canceled the *mehmooni* this week.

Something about not knowing
must have really hurt him.
Or was it something else,
something we did,
something I did,
that really
hurt him?

It's all my fault.
No. It can't be.
Can it?

Whatever it is, it's not good.
Because not coming to a *mehmooni*
is the Persian cultural equivalent of declaring war.

Canceling is the nuclear option.

For some reason,
Maman Joon doesn't seem that upset.
She said it was her father's rug first,
so she could do with it as she wished.

See, in Iranian culture, almost everything is shared.
Not in the way hippies share, or the way Communists share.
More like everything that's owned is owned by family.

And sometimes, in marriages, Iranians get caught
between the things they owned
(and the people they were)
with their first family
and the things they own
(and the people they are)
with their new family.

It's strange.

To think of Maman Joon and Baba Joon
having their own, older families
before starting ours.

They're just the tip of the iceberg.

An iceberg
that's probably going to melt
in a desert, thousands of miles away from this one,
before I ever get to see it.

A Language Like Music, Part 2

I've been listening to Sammy's CD whenever I'm confused.
Which means I've been listening to Sammy's CD a lot. It helps.
And it's got me thinking . . .

IF
                 Eminem is a modern-day Shakespeare,
THEN
                 What meter is he writing in?

I can almost hear it.

"The Way I Am"
feels like a poem, feels like a play
where the words are the plot
and they thicken nonstop
for five minutes straight.

There's so much stress in his stresses.
But they aren't iambic, like Shakespeare's.
Are they? What did Emily say about music
usually having four feet instead of five?

I want to call her. I want to ask her.
But we haven't talked like that in so long.
We don't talk on the phone like we used to.
Those two people we used to be are disappearing.

Anyway — I can't ask Emily about Eminem,
and I've already asked so much of Sammy.

Maybe Ms. Lowell will know?

Anesthetic

"Ba ba bam, ba ba bam, ba ba bam, ba ba bam."

I'm speaking gibberish in Ms. Lowell's classroom at lunch.
And she's listening intently. Not at all caught off guard
by the silliness of the situation.

Which makes me feel a little less embarrassed.

"So yeah —
is that anything?
Like is that a meter?
Like the way iambic pentameter is?"

"Oh, I see what you mean. Could you do it again for me?"

So I do.
And she joins in
with her own version
like she's done this before.

"Da da dum, da da dum, da da dum, da da dum —
unstressed, unstressed, stressed.

Yes! That's anapestic tetrameter!
It's usually used in children's rhymes.
Where did you hear it, Omid?
Is it somewhere in *Midsummer*?"

"No. Actually it's on a CD
my friend Sammy made me."

"Really?"

"Yeah. I think Eminem uses it,
for like, a whole song.
It's really impressive."

"I bet it is! You know rap and poetry share lots of rules,
and the best artists know those rules so well
they can bend or break them at will."

"That's pretty cool.
So, you said it was called
anesthetic-tetra-meter?"

Which is what I had heard her say,
"anesthetic," like the thing a surgeon uses
to numb you before they cut you open
and try to make everything better.

Ms. Lowell laughs.
"I like that, Omid.
I like that a lot. But no,
unfortunately, it's anapestic,
not anesthetic."

"Got it. Not anesthetic . . ."

I laugh too. I guess
sometimes you can say
the wrong thing,
and it's okay.
More than okay.

It's actually the way
to get closer, to get better.

It's the way you learn.

"Anapestic. Thanks."

"Do you like listening to rap?"
"Yeah. I really do."
"Well, I can't say I've kept up much since college,
but what I used to love about rap is the way
some rappers use internal rhyme."

"What's that?"
"It's a line of poetry, or rap,
where certain words rhyme inside each line
instead of just at the end."

"Sounds impressive."
"It is. I bet you've already heard it
without even knowing. Some of the best rappers
can do it without you even noticing.
Listen for it the next time
you're listening to Eminem."

"I will . . . Thanks again, Ms. Lowell."

"Anytime."

Hypnotize Me

That afternoon I tune in to Sammy's CD
for what must be the thousandth time,
listening intently for internal rhyme,
like Ms. Lowell suggested.

And she was right.
It's everywhere.

Have you ever loved something
but not known why?

That's how I felt
about the song "Hypnotize"
by The Notorious B.I.G.

I've listened to it over and over
but can only catch bits and pieces of the story,
like when Farsi is flying by me too fast.

There's a bunch of bragging.
There's lists and lists of luxuries.

(Amidst the lists,
there's a line
about having sex
on "rugs that's Persian"
that I did *not* expect.)

There's definitely a sense that he's here to say
that he's here to stay. That he's the best.
That he's special.

But here's the thing I'm realizing
somehow just now:
every other word
is a rhyme.

And it gives the whole song
an aura. A bit of magic. A flow.
Like a literary abracadabra.

Then the chorus kicks in
where a woman sings

>   over and over
>   and over about
>   how she's being
>   hypnotized
>   by Biggie's
>   words.

And that's when I get it:
he wrote this specific song
in this specific way! On purpose!

He did it for a reason.

>   Every single one of those internal rhymes
>   are proving his point
>   are casting a spell
>   are power and skill
>   are surprising
>   are hypnotizing.

That's why I love it.

Resuscitation

There's a line in A Tribe Called Quest's "Check the Rhime"
where Phife Dawg tells Q-Tip to play the "resurrector"
before he raps his verse, as if Q-Tip can speak
for all the people who came before him,
all the ones who no longer have a voice.

And that line makes me think about words
in a way I've never thought about words before.

Our words can bring life to the dead.
Like speaking is some sort of CPR.
Like it's a resuscitation.

Which is a word that comes from Latin, by the way.
Sucitare means to raise up.
Re means again.
Raise up, again.
Raise them
up, again.

All the dead.
All the poets and playwrights — but also —
All the ones no one ever remembers.

Maybe even the martyrs who died so I could be here.

I listen to Phife as Quince
casting Tip as Resurrector.
And I become Bottom again,
wanting to play
all the parts.

Waiting For The Clouds To Part

"Let me play the resurrector too?"
I imagine myself
begging Phife Quince
or Peter Dawg
as Omid The Weaver.

And then I wait. For an answer.
Patiently. I wait. For someone.

I wait for the clouds
to part and a voice
from above
be it Phife
or Quince
or God
or Sammy
or Mr. Thompson
or Mom
or Dad

to allow me
to command me
to use my voice.

I wait. For a really long time.
Until I know for certain
that there's nothing coming.
Until I know for certain
that I'm all alone.

What if I could cast myself?

Who would I play?
What would I say?

What if I gave
life to our dead?

What if I spoke about Baba Joon's sister?
About how much he missed her?

No.

I don't think that's right.
I just met my grandparents.
I can barely talk to them,
let alone speak for them.

I Want To Sing

like Baba Joon,
but I can't.

I want to speak
like Baba Joon,
but I can't.

But maybe, just maybe,
there's something
I can do.

16 Bars On Being Omid Soltani

Confused / obtuse / I'm feeling removed
from the old me I was / I want to improve
the Omid I am / a new point of view
could I be a man with a plan who can't lose?
my family's lost / so much over time
at times I can't tell / if their pain is mine.
at times I don't know / at times I get scared
at times I can see that the world is unfair
and I hate it. sounding so bleak.
sounding so silent. sounding so weak.
put pencil to paper / a tongue around sound
I'll discover a beat that can turn us around
see something / say something / you're gonna be
amazed by all the ways I say and see
it's really outrageous and really okay
cuz this is a role that I'm willing to play.

So. That's a Rap.

And I don't think
it was all that
bad . . . ?

But I wrote it — so I can't tell.

Maybe
I'll ask Sammy
what he thinks.

Maybe
I'll try to write another one,
an even better one,
to show him.

Bigger Than Both Of Us

It's Friday night, I'm back at Sammy's,
and I brought a brand-new rap
folded up in my back pocket.

I wait till late, till we're done with dinner,
out of parental earshot
and back in his room.

Then I ask Sammy if I can perform something for him.

"You mean, like from your play?"
"Nah. I've been listening to that CD you made me,
like a lot, and I thought, maybe I'd give it a shot?"
"Give what a shot?"
"Writing a rap."

Sammy looks surprised. Sammy looks confused.
Sammy looks the way I must have looked when
we were playing *Blitz* and he suddenly decided
to switch teams.

"You wrote a rap?"
"Yeah, I think. Something like that."
"Sure. Go for it."

So I stand up and rap what I wrote.

> "I'm wading through these words
> worth their weight in gold
> weighing down my thoughts
> waiting to take hold

                    a key for every lock
                    a window for a rock
                    a prayer for a god
                    a Biggie for a Pac

                language is fluttering in my gut
                it's marrowed in my bones
                it's trying to burst out of me
                in public and at home

                the home I ran away from
                when I was very young
                the home I ran away from
                on the tip of my own tongue

                I still miss every syllable
                each one took its toll
                to leave behind a tongue
                means never being whole"

There's silence as Sammy takes
a second to digest.

I think I stumbled on that line I hate,
"in public and at home."
That line is stupid, it doesn't even make sense,
I should have changed it
before I shared it.

But still,
if we sit here just a bit longer . . .
He's gotta say something, right?

"So — what did you think?"

"Pfft." He smirks.
"How many Iranian dudes you see out there rapping, bro?"

I want to say,
"What?"

I want to say,
"Who cares about that? What about the — words?"

I want to say,
"How many black dudes you see out there
working at Abercrombie, bro?"

But I don't.
I'm no renegade.

Instead, my eyebrows climb up my forehead
like they're trying to escape my face.
And I force a smile. And a nod.

Because I know he's right.
I know there's something in the room
that's bigger than both of us,
and it won't let me be me
or Sammy be Sammy.

I know it's huge and horrifying and has to do with the news
my dad watches on TV about the way black people die
and the way black people live. But it also has
to do with the towers falling in New York City
and the *Midsummer* cast list. I know it controls

the way we communicate, the words we call each other,
words like dude and bro and man and *joonam* and *baba*
and bud and *azizam* — and desert dweller and the N-word too.

I know it's the reason Sammy gave me that CD
like it was some kind of map to a treasure
he might be hunting for himself.

I know it's why Sammy tries so hard at baseball
and why I've never seen Baba Joon happier
than he was on that hike.

But I still don't know
what it means
for me.

The Mehmooni Debut

On Sunday after dinner, instead of listening to more poems
or prayers or watching more of Amir's party tricks,
I tell my family I have something to share.

I stand up. No one knows
what I'm about to do.

I'm scared.

But then I imagine
        the man from Sammy's CD . . .
        live from Tucson, Arizona . . .
        passing me a mic.

    "Tenses never really made me feel this tense
    I'm stressed / really don't know / which tense is best
      obsessed / with tenses / they express intent
      I can speak a little Farsi but it won't relent
        I stumble over words / I reach / I fall
    don't know the old language / don't know it at all
     each sentence a banquet / no clothes for a ball
   with big things to say but my words are too small
  there's nothing quite like it, the look in their eyes
  when I loop our conversation for the fiftieth time
I've used up all my how are you's and I'm doing fine's
they want to know me better but I'm calling for lines
from my parents cuz apparently that's all I can do
    try to run away, hide, retreat out of view
      O why am I like this? How did I lose
    the only part of me that I'm dying to use?"

Silence.

Something about doing this rap in this room feels really — right.
But they're so silent I start to think something's really — wrong.

Until one person starts clapping.
It's Amir. His eyes are wide open
like he's been punched in the gut,

but he's smiling.

Then Mom and Dad join in.
Even Maman Joon is nodding and clapping.
I look around the room: Did Baba Joon like it too?
Did he understand it? Did he understand me?
Where's Baba Joon? I don't see him.
Did he see it? Did he see me?

Then I remember.
We rescheduled tonight's *mehmooni* —
and Baba Joon never showed up.

By Heart

Mom walks over. She gives me a hug.
"That was beautiful, baby."
"Umm. Thanks, Mom."

But that's not all she wants to say.
She's looking at me differently.
Considering her next words carefully.
"Do you know those words by heart?"
"Yeah — of course I do — I wrote them."

"And at school, when you perform Shakespeare,
do you know those words by heart too?"
"Yeah . . ."

I don't know where she's going with this.

"And when you perform those words,
do you close your eyes, like you did tonight?"

Hmm . . . I guess I did have my eyes closed tonight.
I was trying not to think of Sammy's reaction to me rapping,
or the terrifying potential of my family's disapproval.

I was trying so hard not to mess up.

"No — I don't. But Shakespeare's already figured it
all out, so I just have to stand up there and perform.
It's harder with my own words.
I need to concentrate.
I need to get them right."

"You got them all right, *joonam*.
Give your poems the same respect you give his.
When you speak, don't close your eyes.

Keep them open, always.

You have to see people
if you want them
to see you."

Hard 2 Explain

Every time I rap
I feel like I am speaking
Farsi in English.

A Surprise

Dad is at school.

I find him in the front office,
in his crisp silk suit and red tie,
filling the whole place with
the smell of Polo cologne.

I don't usually see him like this.
In the middle of the day.
Fresh.

By the time he gets home,
the tie is usually loosened
or off entirely.

And his eyebrows usually sit lower
on his brow, closer to his eyes,
which are usually tired.

But not right now.

Right now, he's wide awake.
Making small talk with the ladies
behind the desk, casually asking
them to get Amir
out of class too,
please.

He is acting
like this is normal.

Which it very much isn't.

I can't think of one reason
in the whole freaking universe
that Dad would be at school
picking us up early.

The last time Amir and I went home early
was on 9/11, when New York City
was on fire and the world
was falling down, and even then,
Mom was the one to come for us
while Dad stayed at work.

And It's Not Just Me Being Me This Time

Amir must be thinking the same thing,
because the first thing he asks
when we get into Dad's car is,

"Is Mom okay?"

"Yes, *baba*, she's okay.
She's going to be okay."

He says it
like "being okay"
and "going to be okay"
are the same thing.

*"Baba Joon
and Maman Joon
needed her help today, and I can't
pick you up later, so I came early."*
Which is obviously a lie.
A lie I choose to believe,
because I am too scared
to ask for the truth.

What We Don't Know

Mom is home. And Maman Joon is here too.
In the middle of the day? That's weird.
Maybe Dad wasn't lying after all?

They're both sitting on the couch, not speaking,
and there's tea on the table,
untouched.

Mom sees Amir and me and opens her arms wide
as if she's asking for a hug.

If my grandparents needed Mom's help,
then why does it look like she's the one
who's been crying?
And if my grandparents needed Mom's help,
then where is Baba Joon?

So I ask her. "Where's Baba Joon?"

She looks up at my dad,
disappointed. He shrugs,
embarrassed,
and shakes
his head.

Then she looks back at me
and says something
that doesn't make
any sense:

"We don't know."

Baba Joon Is Gone

Gone.   GONE?

How
is he gone?   where did —
where did he go?   on a hike?
                on a trip?
Look for the flags
                              made of toothpicks
look for your way   back
             a path   look for the dice
and roll
             get all your pieces
                              back home
back home Baba Joon
       I'm still here

             Be strong for Mom

Did we borrow   her dad?
   Can we borrow   him back?

Why why   why would   he leave?

Oh god
   is he dead?

I lost him   I can lose him
       before   again

She's lost him . . . AGAIN?

286

        Be strong for Mom

Call the police   we need the police   to find
    him   please find him   is there a reward?
                                        is there a list?

LOCAL MAN MISSING
    Stepped out of a picture frame off a plane
and   onto a   carton of   milk   or yogurt   or   sour cream
                         sheer!   *mahst!*   *khameh!*

He couldn't just leave
Maman Joon.

Did he just leave
Maman Joon?

Maman Joon, Part 2

I hug her hard.

She is still strong, but

in this moment, no longer feels safe.

No longer feels solid,
             full of everything
             a parent should be
             full of.

I hold her tight
and sway us both
from side to side.

It's the way I tell her
how much I love her.

Search And Rescue

Dad calls
search and rescue
to report a missing man.

Then he makes a plan,
and we set off.

Amir, Dad, and I,
armed with Baba Joon's picture
framed in our arms,

head to their neighborhood
and their grocery store
and Sabino Canyon, even.

We ask everyone
if anyone
has seen this man?

The one who's cracking
jokes in the middle
of the airport,
surrounded
by family.

I learn to recognize the face
of someone who is about to
tell you no.

Everywhere we go,
Baba Joon is missing.

Thanksgiving

We don't do Thanksgiving this year,
at least not the way we had planned.

It's not some big celebration of being together at last.
With Baba Joon gone, we have Maman Joon over.
There's food, but Mom doesn't make a turkey,
so we don't have one. We barely eat
what we do have (which is
a Persian-style macaroni
I usually love).

No one is hungry.

Knots

Dad knows how to use his words.
Accented and abrupt as they are,
he's built our everything with them.
Selling people rugs they don't need,
by telling them whatever they do.

He's learned the parts of people
like he's learned the parts of a rug.
He knows how certain parts (of people)
react to certain parts (of rugs). For instance,
he knows that some people
just don't like the fringe.

So he tells them what they need to hear:

"Did you know the fringe is the most important part
of the rug? The fringe is a reminder of the rug's time
on the loom. It is the skeleton of the rug.
We call it the warp.
The warp gives structure and support for the pile,
which is the series of beautiful knots that make the whole.
Did you know the tighter those knots are woven,
the higher the value of the rug?
Of course you did, an informed rug buyer like yourself
knows to inquire about knots per square inch!
But did you know that of the tens of thousands of knots
that make up this one-of-a-kind rug,
the most important knots of all
are the ones on the fringe?
Without those bigger bulky knots,
the beautiful small colored knots

would simply fall off the warp,
and the whole rug
would unravel."

It's been a little over a week since Baba Joon left.

And now we know he left, like, chose to,
because one night we realized he took
his suitcase with him.

He chose to plan, to pack up,
     but not to write us
     a note?
He chose to leave, to flee,
     but not to care about
     his family?
I don't understand why
     I'm angry with Baba Joon.
I don't understand why
     I'm grateful for Baba Joon.
I don't understand why
     I miss Baba Joon.

Mom is asking Dad in the kitchen:
How could he just go?
Why is this happening?
What should she do?

Dad tries to help, but he has no answers.
At least none that are good enough for Mom.
Dad doesn't like not being good enough for Mom.
He finally turns to her and says,

*"You know this all
might be for the best . . .
I don't think your father
ever really wanted to live here."*

Mom was warped before.
But after Dad said that,
she unraveled.

I hear yelling from my bedroom and run down the stairs.
In the kitchen, Dad is on his back on the ground.
Mom is on top of him, her arms flying back behind her head
then forward toward his face.
My legs stop working.
I stop working.

Amir pushes past me.

He's grabbing Mom,
pulling her off Dad.
Mom is saying she's sorry,
not to Dad, but to Amir.

Dad turns his head toward me.
He is crying. Through his tears,
he sees his oldest son
stuck.

A boy
made entirely of
tightly woven
knots.

The Poem I'm Afraid To Write

Roses are red.
Violets are blue.
Persians don't divorce.
But Americans do.

The Person On The Phone

One ring, then two, makes me move
to the phone.
I just need
anywhere else
to be.

"Hello?"
"Hey."

I try to make out the sound of the voice,
but there is a war behind me.

"It's me. You okay, Omid?"

Emily.
Oh my god.
It's Emily.

"Oh, hey. Yeah! I'm . . . fine."

Home is broken open,
shattered into sharp shards,
but hearing her voice again feels so good.
I wish Emily was the person in person
that she is on the phone.

"You don't sound normal."

She's finally figured it out.
I'm not normal.

"It's been a weird night. My rents just had a fight."
A brawl might be more accurate. But my tongue tenses,
and my brain trembles as I try to aim my words.

Why did I even tell her?
It's been so long since she called.

"Oh no. I'm sorry. Was it bad?"
"Um, I think so."
"That really sucks, I know how it is . . ."
She does?
"You do?"

"Yeah. But — hey, listen, I wanted to call because Sarah told me
she might have said something to you at rehearsal . . .
like a while ago?"

Whoa. My heart skips a beat.
It feels like forever since that rehearsal.
So long, I almost forgot I don't know
how Emily feels about it.
How she feels about us.

"Oh — about that — yeah — "
"She just — well — I think — "

Just then, Amir runs in begging me
for help with Mom and Dad.

"Hey, sorry, Emily, I actually
think I gotta go. I'm really sorry,
but I'll see you at school tomorrow."

What Men Do

I'm walking into the cafeteria
with Sammy during lunch
just as Emily is heading out.

She's with Sarah, history homework in hand.
Our eyes meet, and we share a super-quick smile.
I start to think maybe that's a good sign.
I start to hope I see her again, soon.
Sammy and I grab our food,
then find a table for two.

Sammy must have seen the smile.
"If you don't move a little faster,
you're gonna get friend zoned, dude,"
he warns me, as if people in love aren't friends.

Isn't that the first step?
Shouldn't it be? What's the other way, even?
Surprise girlfriend! Surprise boyfriend!
That seems absurd. But what if he's right?

"I saw the hearts on your CD, Omid.
Just go for it already. You gotta kiss her.
The longer you wait, the harder it'll get."

He doesn't know the half of it.
Literally.

He might have seen those hearts,
but he hasn't seen what I've seen,
and I never told him about any of it.

About the party and the real reason
I left. About rehearsals after school
and the way she looks at Geoff.
How I saw them holding hands
at rehearsal but didn't know
if they were still acting.

Should I tell him?
Why would I?

Sammy's got that superpower
where whatever he says actually happens,
and maybe that could help me out right now.
Maybe he really is always right, and maybe
that's more important than what I saw
at some dumb party. Or at rehearsal.
What if Emily really is
just waiting for me?

I remember a scene from rehearsal.

Kate yelling after Robbie,
as Helena yelling after Demetrius,
"We cannot fight for love as men may do.
We should be wooed and were not made to woo."

Maybe it's true?
Maybe it's on me
to do what men do.

I mean, how often are
Sammy and Shakespeare
gonna agree?

Before I Know It

I'm walking toward Emily,
who's sitting in the dry grass with Sarah,
near our lockers.

Her CD is playing in my head.

I arrive at my destination
with no idea
what comes next.

"Hey, Emily. Um. There was something
I wanted to say on the phone last night
but couldn't. Can we talk for a sec?"

Emily looks at Sarah
like they were in the middle
of something important.

"Sorry," I say, starting to wonder
how dumb I'd look if I just turned around
and walked away.

But Sarah nods, and Emily turns to me and says,

"Sure. Of course. What's up?"

Without Thinking

She gets up and, without thinking,
I start walking toward the mesquite tree,
toward that blue picnic table,
where we first rehearsed
our audition.

She asks me what I wanted to say,
and I make some excuse
about why I can't tell her yet.
I know there are words coming out of my mouth,
but I can't quite make out what they are.
I'm awake, but I'm moving like I'm asleep.
I'm stuck in slow motion.
My body is on autopilot.

"Is everything okay
with your folks?"

My folks. Their fight.
That's right. She knows.

"I think they're just working
through some things, maybe,
and last night it got a little out of hand,
but I'm probably making it
all sound worse than it is.
You know me. Just worrying.
Just me being me."

We round the corner and see the tree.
I sit on the bench with my back to the table.

Emily sits beside me. Not across.
She chooses to be close to me.
"You don't have to do that, Omid.
You don't have to blame yourself
for what other people do or say."

This is what Emily does
that blows me away.
She sees me, how
I really am.
She sees it all
and, somehow,
still cares.

"My parents fight too, a lot,
and I know how it feels
when it goes somewhere
it's never gone before.
You wonder, at first,
if you're blowing it
out of proportion, but you're not.
You know what you heard.
You know what you saw."

She's right. I do know what I saw.

"Em, it's been really hard being at home
ever since my grandpa left."

I swallow and look up toward the sky,
toward the sun, until my eyes can't take
it anymore. I haven't told anyone at school
about Baba Joon.

"Your grandpa left? Where'd he go?"
"Um, yeah. That's the thing. We don't know.
He's just . . . missing."
"What?! When did this happen?"
"About a week ago. Right before Thanksgiving.
I thought he'd be back by now,
but he's not."

"Wow. I'm so sorry, Omid.
That's — I didn't know. I had no idea.
Is that what you wanted
to tell me?"

She is genuinely concerned.
She puts her arm around me
and places her hand
on mine.

I shake my head. "No, actually —
I wanted — "

This is it. This is the moment
I've been waiting for
for so long.

I turn my hand over
to hold hers.
Then I lean in
and kiss her.

First Kiss

Of all the ways
I ever dreamed
my first kiss might go —

I never thought it'd be like this.

I never imagined
I wouldn't be
kissed back.

Not All Boys

"Not all boys are like you, Omid.

I don't want to mess this up.
I don't want to mess us up.
Why can't we just be friends?

You're my best friend."

So that's what this is?
So that's what this is.

"I'm your — best friend?"

"Yes. Omid. You are. You're kind.
You're thoughtful — and smart — and so — sweet.
You're funny and full of surprises.
You're the person I call
when I don't know
what to do.

You're the person I trust the most."

"But — no — what if that's not
what I *want* — to be?"

"Well, what do you *want* then, Omid?"
Emily squints and shakes her head,
like she's having trouble understanding.
Like we're not speaking
the same language
anymore.

I want to tell her the truth.

I want to tell her that the whole world feels like it's falling
apart, except when I'm around her. That all I want
is to say, "I love you."

But I can't.

Not after a failed kiss,
a kiss we didn't even share.
I can't lose her too.

After all this time together,
I have to believe —

"You know what I want."

But she doesn't. She doesn't know what I want.

"So you really are
just like the other boys,
aren't you?"

The Bell Rings

and lunch ends
before I can
explain.

A Hard Thing To Say, Part 2

"I love you"
is a harder thing to say
when you mean it
but you're also thinking,
"Please love me too."

After School

I try to write her
a letter. Maybe
that would
be better.

Dear Emily

I could be
a version of me
you could love.

After school

I try to write her
to make her
a promise.

Dear Emily

I will be
taller, thinner,
bigger, and stronger.

After school

I try to write her —
but end up throwing away
everything I write to

Dear Emily

The Whole Weekend

I wonder what Emily is doing.
I wonder if Emily knows
what to do.

I keep thinking about what she said:
"You're the person I call
when I don't know
what to do."

The whole weekend

I wait
for Emily
to call

like I wait
for Baba Joon
to come back

but they never do.

My Dad Said Something

about America and about Iran
about the struggle and about the wars
about power and about people
about the things he's seen
and the things he thinks
about his life.

My dad said something
to his friend Bob
to a man he once likely
needed to impress
to a man who once likely
represented some test
that my dad thought
he had passed.

My dad was convinced
that he's safe, that he's in,
that the people around him
love him for him,
that his freedom to speak
was American
like his store
and his taxes
and his gym
and his dream.
But today, his America
tore at the seams.
The FBI called
asking for leads.

"We've gotten reports.
You've said a few things,
anti-American.
Are you guilty or arrogant?
Don't let it happen again.
If you see something
say something . . .
We'll talk to you then."

The FBI called my dad.

My dad? MY dad,
who can bend language
like a wire hanger, who knows
how to use his words, who built
our everything with them . . .

The FBI called my dad,
because of something he said.

I Wish This Was Some Stupid Movie

with some dumb plot. But it's not.
This is how it really happens.

If we open our mouths
or follow our hearts
or tell the truth.

It backfires or boils over or blows up
into some massive misunderstanding.

On Monday

Emily sits all the way across the room
in English class. As far from me
as she could be.

Winners And Losers

I skip lunch with Sammy and wait by her locker.
She's usually out here swapping homework with Sarah.

I know Emily.

I know if she just gives me a second of her time,
if she just stops avoiding my eyes,
I can explain
how there's been
some misunderstanding.

But she doesn't come —
and I know
I've lost.

But lost what?
What was there to win
besides something I wanted
that maybe she never did?

And if I lost,
then who won?

That's when I lock eyes with Geoff.

Geoff Sterling,
who is playing my part in the play,
who hangs out with Emily every day,
who is walking over here right now.

What Geoff Knows

"Hey, Omid."
"Hey."

I pretend to be looking for something in my locker.
But Geoff just stands behind me. Waiting. So I say,
"If you're looking for Emily, she's not here."

"Yeah, no — I know. I was actually wondering
if you and I could talk for a sec?"

Could we talk for a sec?
Can I just say no?
What do you have to say to me, Geoff?

I turn around, and I look at him,
and I realize I've never talked
to Geoff one on one.

All of a sudden, I wish I hadn't skipped lunch with Sammy.

"Yeah, sure, what's up?"
"Listen, I have no reason to believe you're a bad dude.
I know you were one of Emily's first friends here."
"Okay . . . ?"
"But whatever is going on right now . . .
you just have to lay off for a bit.
You can't be hanging around
her locker for all of lunch."

"This is my locker, actually, Geoff."
"You know what I mean, dude."

"No, I don't know what you mean."
"Look, I'm here to make sure you give her
some space. And if I were you, I'd give her
some time to think things through."

"What 'things' exactly?
Did Emily ask you
to talk to me?"

What does Geoff know?

"No — she didn't ask me —
I'm just trying to help."
"Well, maybe you should stop
trying to help. Maybe you should
mind your own business."

"Maybe you should stop
kissing random girls at school."

Emily.
    Isn't.
        Some.
            Random.
                Girl.
Wait.
    Wait.
        Wait.
            Wait.
                Wait.

                        Emily told him?

What Geoff Doesn't Know

is just how easy it is being Geoff.
Not that being anyone is a breeze,
but it's definitely easier
being Geoff.

> Easier than being Omid at rehearsal.
> Easier than being Baba Joon at a grocery store.
> Easier than being Reza fixing windows at 3 a.m.

Geoff always makes the right choice
because Geoff can do no wrong.
He can connect,
can be seen,
he can speak
and convince
the whole world
he's normal.

Why is Geoff
the one who gets
to be normal?

While I'm the one
who has to balance worries
about being different,
too different,
or not different
enough?

Maybe it's just luck.

Luck he was born where he was born when he was born.
Luck his parents have lived in Tucson a lot longer than mine.
Luck he's known his grandparents for as long as he's been alive.
Luck no one wonders how his parents can afford that house.
Luck he's not fat, has never been lapped, never been laughed at.
Luck no part of him has ever been lost in translation.
Luck the FBI has never called his home.

But the thing that makes luck so lucky
is that luck can't last forever.

It can't always be
so easy being Geoff.

Not if I have anything to say about it.

But I Have Nothing Left

to say.

So I curl my fingers back into my palms
and lock them into place
with my thumbs.
I drop one shoulder
and let some part of me fly

away
      from
            me

            and
      right
into

            Geoff Sterling's face.

Soft

At first I forget how to breathe
or how to love or how to protect soft things.
Instead I seek them out, the soft bits, on Geoff.
Even lanky Geoff has soft bits, like lips, and eyes, and balls.
And I try to find them all. Hurt them. Smash them. I try, hard.

But there's a lot more soft on my body than his.
There's more to be smashed on me.
I think I've got the problem
of a soft heart too.

I touched something wet. His eyes or his mouth.
I probably shouldn't have done that.
I probably shouldn't have done any of this. But I did.
And he's better than me. At fighting, too.
At making the whole world bend.

Now someone is bleeding,
and I don't know if it's me or him
or both, or how to end a fight
once you've broken skin.

Intermission

But I don't have to learn,
because Mr. Thompson shows up
and pulls us apart.

Hollow

For so long,
I worried, and wondered, and wandered through
the thickness of language.

And got Nothing for it.

So I went where words won't go. Where they end.
I went where fists and fights and bruises
and blood reside, where they claim to reign.
Where everything is supposed to be simple.
Where you can be right if you can be strong.

I went Wild.

And somehow ended up
with even less than Nothing.

I ended up Empty.
Poured out into the sand
until I was hollow.

I ended up Stupid.
Out of ideas. Out of all the good and left with the bad —
the things bound to make it worse.

I ended up Broken.
Into parts, into pieces, into something dangerous.

I ended up Angry.
That it didn't make me feel better.
That I ever thought it could.

Unacceptable

This is unacceptable, boys.

UNACCEPTABLE

Headmaster Frankel's office is messier
than I thought it would be.

UNACCEPTABLE

We will not condone split lips
or bloody knuckles in our community.

UNACCEPTABLE

Brad's here as witness,
as bystander, as innocence.

UNACCEPTABLE

It's been brought to my attention that you threw
the first punch, Omid. Is that true?

UNACCEPTABLE

Geoff looks down to hide the grin
peeking through his bloody cheap pout.

UNACCEPTABLE

I don't know. I don't know. I don't know.

UNACCEPTABLE

What led to your abhorrent behavior?

UNACCEPTABLE

I don't know. I don't know. I don't know.

UNACCEPTABLE

He's been bothering our friend, making her
feel uncomfortable, says Brad, by far
the biggest man in the room.

UNACCEPTABLE

Why do we call the principal a headmaster
in a school where most boys wear
cargo shorts and flip-flops?

UNACCEPTABLE

I just asked him to stop, Geoff testifies.

                        UNACCEPTABLE

                    I'm shaken like my mom.

               I'm impervious like my dad.

UNACCEPTABLE

No. He punched me first. I lie but am rising.

UNACCEPTABLE

Mr. Thompson cuts me down. It's not true, he says.

He saw the whole thing. He's here too?

                        UNACCEPTABLE

              The four walls are closing in,

          each one conspiring against me.

                        UNACCEPTABLE

                Disappointing. I am the

         disappointing disappointment

               in the room. I am

UNACCEPTABLE

Behavior considered criminal

beyond the borders of our school

is an expellable offense, is

UNACCEPTABLE

But we believe in second chances here.

We believe in redemption.

UNACCEPTABLE

A three-week suspension. That should be enough

time for you to reflect on your actions, Omid.

UNACCEPTABLE
I wonder what the man bought
at the grocery store. The one
who grabbed my mom and
called her a bitch.

UNACCEPTABLE
Go to your locker and pack up your books.
We will expect you to keep up
with your work from home.

UNACCEPTABLE
I can hear my dad's back breaking in the distance.
It booms and echoes across town, shattering
every window in its path.

UNACCEPTABLE
Mr. Thompson is alarmed.
He whispers in Headmaster Frankel's ear.
Something is being begged on my behalf.

UNACCEPTABLE
There will be no exceptions made,
the master commands.

UNACCEPTABLE
Omid, you will give up your role in the school play.

The Whole World Has Exploded

Everything I wanted to do right
has turned out terribly,
terribly wrong.

First Baba Joon,
then Emily,
and now Bottom.

All gone.

All my fault.

I've brought shame
upon the family name,
and when we got home
Mom and Dad just —
grounded me.

Grounded me?
That's it?

I think they're tired.
I think they're out of ideas, too.
I think they're putting their problem away
in a room and are praying he disappears
if they don't look at him.

I Wonder If My Parents Are Giving Up On Me

I wonder what Baba Joon would say if he was still here.

I wonder if he'd be proud that I finally stood up for myself.

I wonder if that's what I was doing.

I wonder if I'm making the mess even worse.

I wonder if I'm doing the opposite of what he would have wanted.

I wonder why he couldn't just laugh along.

I wonder if I'll ever learn to play backgammon now.

I wonder why he left me here to wonder all of this alone.

Sammy Says

"Your parents told me I only get thirty minutes with you."

Sammy is sitting on my bed.
I'm sinking deeper and deeper
into my mom's old office chair,
spinning around in circles at my desk.

"I'm honestly surprised they let you in.
They were pretty pissed yesterday,
promised me I'd be alone in here
for as long as it took me
to realize what I've done."

I'm getting dizzy. I stop spinning and roll over to the mirror.

"Well, they didn't wanna let me in. But I convinced them."

There's Sammy's way with words again.

"Told them I didn't see you
after the fight yesterday. Told them I was worried,
and I had to make sure you were okay."
"You didn't have to say all that."
"Yeah, I did. Cuz it's true."

I look at Sammy behind me, through the mirror.
It's 3:30 p.m. He has his backpack and duffel bag with him.
Which means he must have skipped baseball practice to be here.
Which means he won't get to play in this weekend's games.
But I don't get the sense that he's thinking about baseball.
I get the sense that he's thinking about me.

And I'm about to say I'm okay
when he says,

"Bro. You look like shit."

I laugh, cuz he's right.

"What the hell happened with Geoff?"
"I took your advice."
"My advice? What advice?"
"I kissed Emily."

"Oh — "
                    "And she told him."
                                        " — fuck."
"Yup."

                            We take a moment of silence.

"So are they, like, together?"
"I don't know, man. I guess? All I know is she told him
about the kiss — and then he came over
and started lecturing me by our lockers
like he was doing her some huge favor."
"That's so . . . out of the blue."

I guess there's nothing left to lose.
I might as well tell
Sammy what I saw.

"I mean, yeah — but no too —
not completely out of the blue.
I had a feeling something was going on with them.

329

Ever since the party. I saw Emily sleeping on Geoff's bed
that morning. And then they were holding hands at
rehearsal once a few weeks later."

"Omid.   Wait.   What?

                                                 Why didn't you tell me that?"

"Because —
because I wanted this
to be different."

"Dude, I would have given you some other advice . . .
Sometimes people are just gonna like who they like."

"No. Not just Emily.
Not just Geoff.
I wanted all of it —
everything —
to be different.
And this was supposed to be the year!

The year I got grandparents and maybe a girlfriend,
got free from Amir and even you and there'd be a new
version of me to cover up the old one.

This was supposed to be — I just wanted — "

I stop talking,
because my feelings were turning into words
faster than was doing anyone any good.

                                                         Or so I thought.

"What was wrong with the old one?"
"What do you mean?"

"Since you want a new version of Omid so bad,
what was wrong with the old one?"

Is this some kind of trick?
Is he really going to make me say it?

"I mean, I was just — lame. I was a loser
who never had anything to say about anything.
And even when I did, I didn't know how to say it right."

Sammy makes a face that says,
"How could you say that
about my best friend?"
Then he actually says,

"I always liked it.
I always thought you only spoke when you needed to.
And when you did speak, it really meant something."

There's a knock on the door.
"Sammy, it's time for you to go."

"Okay, Mrs. S — just one more minute!"

Then he turns to me and lowers his voice.
"Listen. I liked the old Omid. Sorry if I never made that clear.
And this new Omid — with the bruises and the bloody lips —
I can like him too. If that's what you want."

I don't think Sammy is actually asking me to make a choice.
I think Sammy is trying to be supportive.
I've never seen him quite like this before.
Sammy looks kinda uncomfortable,

and for the first time,
at a loss for words.

Until finally, he says,

"'Wading through these words . . . worth their weight in gold . . .
weighing down my thoughts . . . waiting to take hold . . .'

Those lines from your rap — that's — it's how I feel too.
Anytime I listen to Biggie or Tip or Nas.
I just didn't expect — after just a couple
weeks with a CD — rapping is
so hard, dude, and —

You're really good, Omid."

I can't believe Sammy just quoted
something I wrote.
I can't believe
he actually
liked it.

Sammy gets up and opens his backpack.
"So yeah — I made you another mix.
I figured you're gonna have some time on your hands
and you might wanna use it to dig into some new verses,
some N.W.A., some Wu-Tang. Dude. You're gonna love it."

He tosses me a new CD.
"Stay out of trouble. Expect you back in action soon."
Then he turns around and heads home.

Simin Is Back

My aunt has been living with Maman Joon since Thanksgiving,
but she's been in our living room since noon.
Dad is home too, for some reason.
I haven't seen him miss this much work, ever.

I'd been lying in bed
listening to Sammy's new CD
until I heard something,
someone yelling.

At first I thought it was some part of the song,
but then I realized it was in Farsi.
I pulled off my headphones quick
and cracked the door to the balcony.
I'm not really allowed to leave my room,
but I can hear what's going on downstairs
a lot better with the balcony door open.
I can't catch everything.

But I can tell it's not Mom or Dad yelling.
It's Simin. Which is super weird,
because she's usually so quiet.
And that's when I hear it:

SIMIN
YOU KNOW DAMN WELL WHERE HE IS, SHOHREH!
MOM
SO DO YOU!

And then my dad's deep voice rumbles.
And then Mom and Simin get real quiet again.

And then the world goes back to being mumbles.

They must be talking about Baba Joon.
I put my head to the floor
and try to listen so hard
my ears start to hurt.

Maybe this isn't the most practical way to listen.
Maybe I like it because it feels like I'm praying.

> *(mumble mumble mumble)*
> ### SIMIN
> *I'm sorry. I'm sorry. But what did you think would happen—*
> *bringing that man all the way out here?*
> *(mumble mumble mumble)*
> ### MOM
> *We can't. We have the kids —*
> *(mumble mumble mumble)*
> ### SIMIN
> *No. Absolutely not. The only place I'm going — is back to our*
> *mom's house — to take care of her.*
> *(mumble mumble mumble)*

> *SIMIN exits.*

I'm so confused.
I need to see for myself.
I head out to the balcony,
pretending I didn't hear anything.
I watch Simin get into her car.

I wave, but she doesn't wave back.

Not Being Able

Mom came to my room tonight.
She had been crying, again.

I am so tired
of not being able
to help.

I told her I was sorry and embarrassed.
That I knew I shouldn't have hit Geoff.
She said that she was sorry too.
And then she said,

"I think Baba Joon is in London.
And I'm going to go get him."

Out Of Order

My heart sank.
My stomach jumped.
And as the two reached out
to touch each other,
I felt it. I knew it.

"Mom.
I can help.
Let me come
with you."

She looked at me,
quiet for a long time.
Like the world was out of order.
Like in some way, she knew it would be better
for her son to accompany her. In some way, I knew it too.
Things hadn't been the same since September,
since that fight in that parking lot
where I saved the day
by calling that son of a bitch "sir."

Finally, she said,

"Okay. You start packing.
I'll talk to your dad."

All At Once

Mom gets up to leave,
and there's a knock at the door.
Amir is standing on the other side
holding the house phone with one hand,
covering the microphone with the other.
"Omid, it's for you . . .
It's Emily."

Emily called.
I feel a sudden rush.

Amir may be willing to help, to buy me some time,
while I figure out how I'm going to make things right.
"Tell her I'm busy?
Tell her I'll call her back soon."
Mom looks back at me, eyebrows raised.
"No. Don't do that. Tell her I'm sorry.
Tell her I'm grounded — and that I'll call her when I can."
Amir nods and heads toward his room.
Mom waits for him to close his door, then says,
"If you need to talk to her, you can."
I feel the rush again,
but now it's becoming pressure,
pressure building up inside me.
It wants to escape.
It wants
to wail.

"Thanks, Mom. I do. But I — can't.
Not right now."

Brothers, Part 3

"What was that about?"
"She probably wants to talk about the fight with Geoff.
I don't wanna deal."

"Are you okay, Omid? For real."
"Yeah, man. Are you okay?"
"For sure."
"Okay. Good."

"I overheard you and Mom talking through the door —
are you actually gonna go to London?"
"Yeah. I think I am."

"Do you think he's really there? Baba Joon?"
"I don't know."
"Mom seems pretty certain about it, but she won't say why."
"I didn't even ask."
"Well — I don't know why he'd be all the way out there."
"Me neither."

"It's weird, right?"
"Everything's been weird lately."

A moment passes.
Amir speaks first.

"I'll miss you."
"I'll miss you too."

Honors English

I walk down the aisle
on the plane behind my mom,
searching for our seats.

We are flying
from Tucson
to Phoenix
to New York City
to London.

I've never been on a trip with just Mom.
I've never been afraid of people praying before takeoff.
I've never been on a plane post-9/11.
I've never made sure

to speak Honors English
as we walked through
airport security.

A security I never knew
we needed.

Layover

There are trains in JFK Airport
that take you from terminal to terminal.
And each New York City terminal
is big enough to fit a whole Tucson airport in.

Maybe that's why I feel so small here.

Those trains can take you into the city, too.
But Mom says we don't have time to explore.

There was a woman on our flight
who pointed out the spot where the towers used to stand
to her daughter as our plane lowered itself to land.

I hope she didn't see me
staring.

I wonder what it would have felt like to live here this year.
I wonder if I'll ever live anywhere
but Tucson.

We find a food court to spend the few hours we have
before we board the flight for London.

The whole place looks like Christmas is coming.
Red and green and mildly merry, but no one is festive.
The holidays put me in the mood for Chinese food,
so I find a place to order orange chicken.

Mom gets noodles and some tea,
and when we're eating and clearly not thinking

about the same thing, she suddenly says,

"Omid joon, I don't understand.
Why did you hit that boy?"

"It was just a stupid fight, Mom.
And I told you already,
I'm sorry."

"But I want to know why you did it."

Why I did it.
                    Like I could explain.
                                        All the reasons.
                    Like I even know.
All the reasons.

"There's a girl. And we both like her.
And I think she likes him
more than she likes me."

That's all I say.

I wait for Mom to make some big speech
to say something about how that's not reason enough
to say something about how fighting is never the answer
to say something about our words and how to use them
to say something anything at all, but all she says is,

"Okay . . .

Okay."

What Mom Said On The Plane

"I shouldn't have done that
the other day, Omid.

To your dad.

I shouldn't have — hit him.

He just always has to say something.
And sometimes I need him to not.
I need him to stop

and listen.

When we were younger,
I listened to him
because he reminded me of home.
Sometimes when you listen long enough —

you fall
                    in love.

He talked and he talked. He loved to talk.
But I don't know if he ever learned
to listen.

Let alone
                    long enough."

What If

I told you earlier
that Dad sells rugs. Well.
That it was his vocation, his answer to a calling,
a predetermined destiny, something like love.

But what if that's not true?

Don't get me wrong. Rugs are important
in Iran. They weave together every vibrant color
of a culture that dates way back before anything
I've learned about in AP US History.

Before muskets and treaties. Before tariffs and Boston tea parties.
Before the trails to Oregon or the ones made of tears. Before
Shakespeare, too. Definitely before 1992, when Disney convinced
me carpets could fly, and I pretended to be Aladdin for two
years in a row on Halloween but also not on Halloween. Before
Dad had to let me down easy, sharing with me a truth, that his
rugs couldn't fly, even though a part of him wished they would,
because I was finally spending so much time with him inside his
store, searching for treasure like it was a cave of wonders.

What if it wasn't all meant to be?
What if our fortune wasn't fated?
What if it happened by accident,
and now we're here, full of knots,
and only sometimes happy?

What if he found himself far away from home in 1979,
with a new wife in a new land
that was freshly painted

but not quite vibrant,
and he just couldn't stand
the idea of anything else new?
What if he chose to spend his time
surrounded by something, anything, he understood?
That was familiar. That he knew about because *everyone*
back home knew about it too.

Maybe it was never meant to be a whole life. Maybe he started doing it for Mom, then me, then Amir, just trying to get by, by sharing what he knew from his old home with the strangers in his new one. Maybe it worked. Maybe he saw Americans start valuing his rugs — seeing things in ways they hadn't before. Maybe he made new friends who were learning the difference between *gabbehs* and *kilims* and wanted one in their home and wanted my dad to get one for them, and that made him part of some small thing he wasn't a part of before and that felt good. Felt more normal. Never letting go of his old home while trying to build a new one.

What if our destiny

is just one change of plans after another?

Maybe

that wouldn't be so bad.

Maybe I don't need to have
every answer right
now.

Maybe,
like Dad,
I'll learn
to adapt.

Customs

We landed in London in the morning.

The sun rose slow,
and the clouds hung low,
keeping the city under cover
till just a few seconds before
we touched the ground.

How was it morning already?

I remember the bright night lights
of New York City dimming. I remember falling
in and out of sleep over a dark bruise-purple ocean
for just a few minutes, maybe twenty, maybe thirty,
but now we're here? The sun is up, and the day is new?

We lost time crossing the world.
Mom says we'll get it back
when we fly home.

I've never been to a foreign country before.
Unless you count Mexico, which I guess you should,
so I guess I have, but even then, I've only been to Nogales,
and a border town doesn't feel too foreign.

When we went to Mexico, we had to wait
in a long line at the border for the agent
to peek into our car and wave us across.
I never knew what they were looking for.
The whole thing seemed so arbitrary.
Who gets in. Who gets out.

I remember my dad was driving,
and I was sitting in the back seat
wishing so hard that he wore reading glasses,
because bad guys never wear reading glasses.

I was a little kid. It made sense at the time.

But there was nothing arbitrary about getting into England.
We had to fill out forms and go through something called
customs before we could even claim our luggage.

Customs was long lines at the border, again,
but this time people were organized
by their country of citizenship.
We stood behind all the other
US Passport Holders.

A man in a military uniform sat
behind his desk,
behind his plexiglass,
behind his dark black mustache,
with no hair on his head. He asked
for our passports and muttered,
"Business or pleasure?"

It took Mom a few seconds to realize
he was talking to us.

"Are you here for business or pleasure, ma'am?"

He wanted to know why we were here,
but the options he offered
were so far from the real reason

we were here that I let out a little laugh.

The man looked down
and over at me.
I imagined his mustache
bristling, moving again.

"Business or pleasure or runaway grandfather?" he'd say.
"Runaway grandfather," I'd say.
"Oh, well, congratulations, lad!
You've come to the right place.
We got loads of 'em," he'd say.
And we'd be on our way
into the land of lost grandpas.

"Pleasure," my mom said.

He looked back at her,
stamped our passports,
and let us in.

"Welcome to London."

We Made Our Way To The Hilton

It should have been easy.
It should have been nothing
to write home about.

Right?

But it wasn't
easy. It was nearly
the end, of everything.

We got out of the cab. I grabbed my bag
out of the back and went to cross the street.

That's when the tires screeched.

I jumped back in disbelief
as a car swerved across the median,
just barely missing me.

I didn't understand.
There hadn't been a car there
a second ago, I swear.

I'd looked before I crossed,
like I've done my whole life,
like I've done a million times before
landing in London.

But that's the thing.
I was in London, in England,
all the way across the world,

where they drive on the left side
of the road. Not the right side
of the road. It was the wrong side
of the road back home.

I'd looked the wrong way.

I was in a foreign land, where they did things differently.
Where I was a stranger who didn't understand
the customs, and it almost killed me.

All I had to do was read the signs.
All I had to do was open my eyes.
All I had to do was try.

But I hadn't.

Because I wasn't used to having to try really hard
to do things that have always been really easy.

The cabdriver got out of his car
to make sure everything was alright.
Mom ran over and hugged me and kissed me
and started yelling about how I had to pay more attention.
But I wasn't paying that much attention. I couldn't.
I was thinking about Baba Joon. Again.
In that grocery store.
Trying, so hard.

And I started to understand,
why someone might want to run
away from all of that.

Black Pudding

Mom was checking in.
I had a brand-new lease on life
(which, it turns out, makes you pretty hungry),
so I wandered toward the waft of a breakfast buffet.

They were almost finished serving.

The only thing left out was something called black pudding,
which did not look like any kind of pudding I'd ever seen.
I mean, not even close. It looked like sausage.

I asked the nearest waiter what it was.

"Right, that's our traditional black pudding."

"What's in it?"

"Well, you've got your barley, oatmeal, onions, pork fat,
and a heaping serving of pig's blood."

Something about the way he said that last part
made me think that telling American kids
what was in black pudding
was one of the few parts of his job
he still enjoyed.

So yeah. England
is going to be weird.

Long Distance, Part 2

We call home from our hotel room
to tell Dad and Amir we've landed.

Mom speaks to Dad for a bit, then says,
"Omid joon, come here.
Baba wants to hear your voice."

I pick up the phone. "Hey, Dad."
"Baba jan! I miss you so much, *baba*!
How was the flight?"
"It was good. I slept most of the way."
"You did? Very good! The first time
I flew across the ocean,
I could not sleep."
The first time Dad flew across the ocean
was when he was moving to America.
"You are a world traveler now, *baba*! Maybe next summer
you can come with me on my buying trips? Nepal?
India? Turkey? Wherever you want to go!"

I notice my dad's voice has gotten louder,
like it always does when he's on the phone,
long distance, with family far away.
Like he's trying to pass a baton across the globe.

I make my voice a little louder too,
to meet him halfway.

"Yeah, *Baba*, maybe next summer."
"Good, Omid *jan*. Good. Wait one minute.
Amir wants to talk to you."

Brothers, Part 4

Amir jumps on the phone
before my dad has even finished his sentence.
"Yo, dude!"

"Sup?"
"Just wanted to see how you were doing.
How was the flight? How's London?"
"The flight was fine. Fast.
Got real tired and missed most of it, honestly.
Seeing New York was pretty weird."
"Yeah. That makes sense."

"But London is cool.
Our hotel serves black pudding for breakfast.
Look it up and tell me if you
want me to bring some back for you."
"Is it just, like, chocolate pudding? Can't we get it here?"
"Just look it up. I think you'll definitely want some
all the way from London."

"Alright, alright. Oh, by the way —
I ran into Sammy today after school.
Apparently, Mr. Thompson asked him to be in the play?"
"What?! Really?"
"Yeah, I mean, Mr. Thompson is definitely looking for someone
to come in and replace you. They open this weekend.
You kinda left them in a bind."

"I guess I did. But that's desperate.
Could you imagine Sammy in a Shakespeare play?"
"Nope. And Sammy felt the same way.

It was a big no from him. But we talked about it for a while.
I asked him what was going on. They really don't have much
time, and pulling in one of the other cast still leaves a hole
in the show. Mr. Thompson doesn't know what to do."

As he fills me in, I notice how enthusiastic Amir sounds.
How invested he is. Maybe he's putting on a performance
for me. Or maybe he already misses me.
Maybe I already miss him too.

Maybe it's a little bit of all the above.

Whatever it is, it feels like we're cracking the case
of the missing mechanical, together. It feels like he wants
my help, or needs a nudge, just like I needed his
when we were running lines. So I say,
"What about you?"

"I mean, I don't know what he should do either."

"No, Amir, what about *you*? You know the lines.
We ran it like a hundred times. You were even
correcting me by the end without looking at the script."

"Umm, bro — I'm not in high school — remember?"
"I bet that doesn't matter to anyone right now.
Think about it. You'd be a million times better
than anyone else who tried to do it."

"But I wouldn't be better than you. You were so good, Omid.
They're gonna expect you — and get me.
I can't do the family name like that."

That's when it hits me. Like truly hits me.
Like rounds the corner and slams into
my unexpecting chest. I'm not in the play.
I'm never going to play Bottom. And I *was* good.
Good enough to have a vision. Good enough to see
a version of him that felt real and honest.
Good enough to know better.

And I lost it.
I lost my one chance
to show everyone
what I'm capable of.

"Omid? You there?"

"Yeah. I'm here. Thanks, man. That means a lot."
I take a moment. I take a breath. And then I say,
"But what I need right now, what the family name needs,
what Mr. Thompson obviously needs, and what
Bottom needs — is you. I think you got this."

This time, Amir is the one who goes silent.

"Amir? Did you hear me?"
"Yeah. But I don't know."

"Well, I do. I know. Will you please promise to at least
ask Mr. Thompson about it at school tomorrow?"

"Yeah, sure."
"You promise?"

"I promise."

Where Is Baba Joon?

I need to do something.
I need to fix something.
I need to fix anything.

"So, should we go find Baba Joon now?"

I ask loudly, watching my mom
unpack a suitcase
for a lot longer
than it should take
to unpack a suitcase.

She shakes her head.

"Let's just take a day
to rest. Let's take a day
to catch our breath."

Catch our breath?

We just planned a trip,
flew across the world,
and landed in London
in a matter of seventy-two hours,
only to wait an entire day before doing anything?

Any kind of clarity I had
on the call with Amir
is officially fading fast . . .

What is going on?

A Friend

The rest of the day was a lesson in "jet lag."
Apparently, the sleep you get in a plane
doesn't work the same way as
the sleep you get in a bed.

I found myself bundled up in a cold country,
wearing my big new winter coat like a blanket . . .
I found myself nodding off all over London.
On the second story of a double-decker bus . . .
Outside Buckingham Palace . . .
Beneath Big Ben . . .

I found myself dipping
in and out of dreamlands
until Mom surprised me by saying,

"I have a friend I want you to meet today.
She's still at work now,
but I thought we could visit.
You might like it."

"You have a friend . . . here? In London?"

"Of course I do, *azizam*.
Your mother is very popular."

She smiled as she hailed us a cab.

The London Bridge

is actually in Arizona.
I'm not kidding. Arizona!
That's the for-real actual truth!

Our driver told us (as we crossed the new London Bridge)
that apparently the old London Bridge, the original, was bought
by an American businessman and transported
to America to some small town
called Lake Havasu,
in Arizona.

Lake Havasu is just a few hours from our house.

He said he's a bit of a "bridge enthusiast,"
and he hopes to be able to travel west
one day to see it.

Mom looked at me, and I looked at her,
our eyes growing wider,
like we were in on some big secret
about how small the world was.

Fariba

We got out of the cab in front of a big white building
that looked like a cross between a kite and a cottage.

It was a building out of place
in a modern metropolis, like it was from another time.

But the lady standing out front was nice enough.

She must have been waiting for us,
because as soon as she saw my mom
she started smiling and couldn't stop.

The two of them hugged
and started catching up
in Farsi.

Then she turned to me
and said in perfect English,

"And this must be Omid."

"Yup. That's me.
Nice to meet you . . ."

Mom jumped in.

"This is Fariba, Omid *joon*.
We grew up together,
a long time ago,
in Tehran."

"Oh yes. A thousand years ago."
Fariba joked and laughed
with Mom in a way that
warmed the space
between us.

I started looking around
at the banners blowing in the breeze
on flagpoles nearby.

One of them had a painting on it
of some guy who looked
a lot like Shakespeare.

Fariba must have noticed me noticing it,
because that's when she said,

"Omid *jan*,
let me be the first
to welcome you to
the Globe Theatre."

The Globe Theatre

We step through the massive doors
as Fariba explains to my mom and me
that she's the "director of development here,
which is just a fancy way of saying that I raise money
for people like Omid to do what they do best."

Fariba gives us a tour and tells us all about
the "rich history" of the site.

I try to listen,
but I'm still in shock.

It takes me more than a minute to register:
I'm in the Globe Theatre.

Shakespeare's Globe Theatre.

I'm standing right in the middle
of his story, which is now
my story too.

This building
is unlike any place
I've ever been before.
It's been closed and reopened.
It's burned down and been rebuilt.
It's not really new and not really old.
It's not quite indoors but not all the way outdoors.
It has a stage and two balconies full of seats
but also an empty open floor where people
can stand, right up front.

Fariba says that the institution survived
because the stories told here
have shaped our world.

My mom eyes the stage.

"Why don't you go up there and do something for us,
Omid *joon*?" my mom asks me, as if they
would just let anyone get onstage
at Shakespeare's Globe.

I look to Fariba so she can explain to my mom
how ridiculous that idea is.

But instead
she says,

"From what your mom tells me,
you're going to end up up there one day.
Why not start now?"

The Weaver's Dream

I'm walking on the stage of the Globe Theatre.
I'm breathing in the same air Shakespeare once did.
I wonder if he was ever scared?
Like I am always.
Like I am now.

The thing about speaking words up on a stage
is that you never know how far they'll go.

They could die in the fourth row,
covered up by a common cough.

Or they might make it
all the way to the back wall,
landing softly, as intended.

Or they may break out of the theater entirely
and never stop traveling across space and time
into the hearts and minds of all
those who've heard them.

I wonder if
he knew?

I wonder if
I can still do it?

All those lines I learned. Before I lost my part in the play,
before I lost my way. The monologue I forgot that day.
Bottom waking up from what he convinced himself
must have been a dream.

This is my chance, to find it,
to find out what I am
capable of.

I can't be scared anymore.

In order to wake up, I have to lie down.
So I lie on the stage and close my eyes. It reminds me
of sleeping on the floor all those months ago in Amir's room.
I start to think how everything that's happened since then
has felt surreal, how, like Bottom, I can't quite believe
the way I ended up here, how none of it
seems true, but deep down, I know it is.
I want to give these words their due.
I want to be Bottom the way *I* want
to be Bottom. Not too big.
Not too funny. Just me.
As real as I can be.

OMID THE WEAVER

When my cue comes, call me, and I will
answer: my next is, "Most fair Pyramus." Heigh-ho!
Peter Quince! Flute, the bellows-mender! Snout,
the tinker! Starveling! God's my life, stolen
hence, and left me asleep! I have had a most rare
vision. I have had a dream, past the wit of man to
say what dream it was: man is but an ass, if he go
about to expound this dream. Methought I was — there
is no man can tell what. Methought I was, — and
methought I had, — but man is but a patched fool, if
he will offer to say what methought I had. The eye
of man hath not heard, the ear of man hath not
seen, man's hand is not able to taste, his tongue

to conceive, nor his heart to report, what my dream
was. I will get Peter Quince to write a ballad of
this dream: it shall be called Bottom's Dream,
because it hath no bottom; and I will sing it in the
latter end of a play, before the duke:
peradventure, to make it the more gracious, I shall
sing it at her death.

There's a clap   and an applause
                 of thunder   of rain

Fariba and Mom run inside for cover
                    but I can't stop, won't stop

I look up
I am up
            I am somewhere
                    between
    Here
and Home
                Lost
            and Found
                            Dreaming
                            and Awake

        Is this really
        happening?

I catch a glimpse
            of a glimmer going all the way back
                    to something holy
                    to musicians
                    who are suddenly sitting

in their box above the stage

They bring out their horns
                                    and play a line
like from A Tribe Called Quest's
                                    "Check the Rhime."

I kick the stage like a drum
                                    it booms
                                                through
                                                            time,
as the past,
                    the present,
                                    and future
                                                align
I look down

people rush the stage ready for a show

  the stands are suddenly packed and

            I find my flow

~ A mic appears onstage, music explodes through the space ~

Omid Raps To A Sold-Out Crowd In The Rain

Helloooooooo, everybody! We're live from the Globe!
Where the microphone is hot and Omid's about to blow, so
all aboard the bandwagon, it's filling up quick,
cuz every time I spit, everybody says it's sick!
Not like vomit (nah!) more like Adonis (yo!)
watch me brace myself / no orthodontist (oh!)

I was admonished, punished, so I left the play
so I left my home with so much left to say,
not the best I confess that I lost my way
till I found myself performing on a London stage
rapping up a storm where the greatest played
which could've never happened if my folks had stayed
at home / in the country they were born in
instead of packing suitcases, forever being foreign,
so I could be old me so I could be new me
so I could be Shakespeare meets Jay-Z and Rumi

Amir Pushes His Way Through To The Front, Proud

Amir! I fear that I led you astray
in doubting myself, might have pushed you away.
Anxiety made me always compare
instead of enjoy all the things that we share.
Bottom is special / I know you can play him,
the lines are important / I know you can say 'em.
You said that you think that I'm paving the way,
but I lean on your lead when I'm starting to fray.
I'm sorry, bro. That is the truth.
I've got a family. You are the proof.

**Emily Appears In The Front Row Of The Second Balcony,
Near The Heavens**

O heavenly Emily! I was so dumb,
you were so good to me, what have I done?
you were the remedy to my dilemma, he
shook you and took you away from me.

— wait —

367

Away from me? Like you ever were mine?
How much of a love is made up in a mind?
Don't know if you hate me don't know if you love me
remember your CD and what you thought of me?
I prayed to your Bright Eyes, and Green Day and Weezer,
auditioned for love, bottomed out as a weaver.
We talked / it touched me / I tried to caress
I took a good thing and I made it a mess,
misread it / that moment I wish I could edit
the way I behaved / I wasn't clearheaded
shortsighted excited I made a mistake,
mistook our friendship, a kiss took its place,
like a punch in the face / it was over so fast
I raced to conclusions and ended up last.

**Baba Joon Walks Out From Backstage
Holding A Bag Of Green Flags**

All of this time my Baba Joon rhymed
with sorrow / he sang / every day was a climb,
a new revolution, a western frontier,
home wasn't home, everything was unclear,
so he left / succumbed to some feeling
he left / his family reeling
he left / but his grandson would chase him
across several nations to finally face him
uncover the clues, make the mystery plain,
why did he leave us and cause all this pain?

Sammy Runs In, He's Sorry He's Late

Sammy, man, do you see what you've done?!

You gave me a push and it taught me to run
laps on laps on laps on laps
on tracks on tracks on tracks on tracks
you're such a real one / you opened my eyes
I pulled an Omid / because of my pride
you knew the old me / you questioned the new
you're always there willing to tell me the truth
you never dropped me / you never exhaust
you helped me wander without getting lost.

William Shakespeare Paces At The Back of the House

Apologies, Will, for using your theater
to parse out my problems in rhyme and in meter.
Took over your stage like I'm taking a page
out your book, see it looks like I've managed to stay
attentive, retentive of all that I've seen.
So maybe *your* words are not all I can be?
It may be absurd but I'm starting to think
that *I* could be the writer
of the story.

~ The illusions fade ~

Omid Is Once Again In An Empty Theater, The Rain Stops Falling

I've spoken, awoken, like Bottom from dreams,
if life be a tapestry, I am the seam,
tactfully weaving together all sides,
I'm rhyming, aligning
along the divides,

I'm standing here swinging, I'm starting to thrive
I'm speaking up, singing
with nothing
to hide.

2 a.m.

I spent the rest of the night
"out on the town" with Mom and Fariba,
watching them find a way to be who they used to be as kids,
and who they are now as adults,
together.

Fariba took us to her favorite pub around the corner,
and we all ordered the "fish and chips."

The fish was fried cod, and chips are what they call fries
in England. But they don't serve them with ketchup,
they serve them with malt vinegar. And I know
that sounds gross, but it was actually so good —
like a breaded *mahi sefeed* served with
a side of french fry *torshi*.

Which reminded me of Maman Joon.
Which reminded me of Baba Joon.
Which reminded me why we're really here.

We got back to the hotel a little while ago.
Mom turned in, but I can't sleep,
cuz before she went to bed
she told me: tomorrow
we'll go find him.

Tomorrow.

Or should I say today?
It's 2 a.m. Right around the time
night becomes morning again.

Mona

It's raining again
as we pull up to an apartment building in a cab
on the wrong side of the road.

Mom buzzes.

A woman older than my mom,
but younger than Maman Joon,
opens the door.

I wait at the bottom of the stairs.
Mom walks up and greets her.

It's another reunion, but not like the one at the Globe.

They're familiar, but something is wrong. Or unwanted?
The woman looks past my mom and sees me.
My mom turns and asks me to join them.
When I do, the woman's eyes widen,
as if, for some reason,
I am dear to her.

"Omid, this is Mona," my mom says.
I smile as she kisses me on each cheek.
Behind Mona, in the hallway,
Baba Joon appears
on the wrong side of the world.

Retreat

Baba Joon sees me first,
his eyes shooting open, even wider than Mona's.
A smile spreads slowly across his paler-than-usual face
as he gasps, "Omid!"

Then he sees my mom,
and his smile
retreats.

What I'd Planned To Tell My Grandfather

You told me you would protect me.

You told me being a good leader means worrying
about the well-being of those who follow you.

You tried to teach me a lesson
you never learned yourself.

I know people your age sometimes wander off.

They get lost.
They take long walks.
They follow some road,
until they forget where they came from,
until someone finds them and reminds them,
until someone helps them home.

But *you* didn't forget
where you came from.

I don't think you even cared.

When *you* wandered off,
you didn't even leave behind any flags.

What I Actually Tell My Grandfather

is not that
perfect.
Is rooted in
the right now,
not a prior idea.
In this face-to-face.
In this wonderful and awful.
In this overwhelmed.
In this real.

What I actually tell my grandfather is,

"Delam barat tang shodeh,"

which technically translates to

"My stomach has tightened for you,"

but actually means

"I miss you."

Persian or English

Our moment together is over
before it really begins.

Mona turns to Baba Joon and says,
"You take your daughter to the other room and talk.
I'm happy to look after Omid."

Mom shoots her a look.

"Please, my dear, today you are my guest, relax.
I'll ask him all about school."

Mom nods and follows Baba Joon through the hallway,
into a room I can't see.

Mona takes me to her living room
and sits me on a black leather couch,
a coffee table
between us.
There is a zebra
skin made into a rug
beneath us.

After a moment she asks,
"Would you like some tea?"
"Sure."
"Okay, I'll make some!"
She gets up to leave the room
the same way we came in.
But then she remembers
to turn and ask me,

"Persian or English?"

"Persian."

She leaves the room, and I call out,
                "With a little bit of honey, if you have it."

The Other Woman

There is art on the walls.
Blue paintings beside blueprints in frames.
There are bookcases filled with books in
Farsi, French, and English.

Like Mona,
this room is clean
and angular.

Some light,
sunlight, hits my eye,
bouncing off a golden picture frame
on the bookshelf, in front of the books
with Farsi on their spines.

I stand up and walk over.

In the frame, there's a picture — color faded, old, vintage,
cool — of two pretty women in swimsuits.
It reminds me of an Abercrombie ad.

The two women are leaning against the trunk of a car
parked by a beach. They are eating cherries out of a glass jar
and laughing about something or someone off camera.

A man is untying four bicycles from the roof of the car.
His back is turned to the camera. His shirt fits him awkwardly.
He's no Abercrombie model.

That's when I realize.

The first woman is Mona.
I didn't notice it right away
because her hair looks different, but her face
is almost exactly the same as it was
when I met her moments ago.

The other woman . . . I don't know.
But she looks familiar.

The license plate of the car is in Farsi.
This must have been in Iran. A long time ago.
When Tehran was Paris.

The other woman . . . is younger than I've seen her before.
In another picture. Another frame. Another place.
At Maman Joon's house as Baba Joon sang
and cried, and oh wow, the man on top of the car
is Baba Joon, but younger, and
the other woman in the picture
is Azadeh, Baba Joon's sister.

Burns

Mona comes back with two cups of *chai*,
served dark, with two cubes of sugar
and no milk (or honey).

She sits. I sit. The first sip
burns my tongue, so we wait
for the tea to cool.

What She Was Going To Be

"What grade are you in, Omid *jan*?"
"Tenth. I'm a sophomore in high school."

"You're in high school? Unbelievable. How time flies.
Do you like it, your high school?"
"It's okay."

"But you are here now with your mom —
are you on winter break?"
"Yeah. Something like that."
"Which subject is your favorite?"
"I don't have one, really."
"Well . . . what are you looking most forward to
when you get back?"

Emily.
I want to say Emily,
but I don't know what will happen
when I go back. I don't know how Emily reacts
to any of this. To my fight with Geoff. To the kiss.
I never called her back. I don't know
quite who I am to her or who she
is to me. I know I messed up.
I know I need to apologize.
But I don't know if she
can forgive me.
So, no.

I don't say Emily.

"I was in the school play."

I surprise myself.
Do I miss that the most?
Maybe I do. I used to
really look forward to it.
But I haven't been happy
at rehearsal for a while.
I'm lost in thought
but get pulled back
into the room when
Mona speaks.

"You know" — she's smiling —
"the last time I saw your mother,
she was about your age — "

"In Iran?"

"Yes, in Iran. She was always in her school plays
and reading poetry at our *mehmoonis*.
We all thought she was going to be
a wonderful artist.
But I hear she's done very well
in America. Your parents have done well, with their business."

I don't know what to say.

"My mom was in plays? And she read poetry?"

"Of course! Didn't you know?"

What Else

don't I know?

Leaving

But before I can find out —
Mom rushes down the hall.

"Come, Omid. We're leaving. Now."

Her voice sounds calm,
but her footsteps on the wooden floor
somehow sound angry.

She stands at the door waiting,
fumbling through her purse.
I walk over to her slowly,
waiting for Baba Joon's footsteps to follow —
but they don't.

"So — is Baba Joon coming with us?"

Mom looks at me
as if something inside her is getting colder.
"Listen to me, Omid. Baba Joon is an adult.
He makes his own decisions.
We came here, we found him,
we told him we missed him,
and now it's time for us
to go home, okay?"

What? Go home? Already? But we just got here.
I feel the knots in me start to tighten.
I feel the need to understand.
I feel a fire in me start to burn.

But then Baba Joon is there,
and I run over to him, and I hug him,
and he hugs me too, so tight,
and I think back to the very first night we met,
back when I thought my family had been made whole,
back when I thought we were on our way to wonderful,
and I realize this might be it . . .
the closest to whole
we ever get.

I start to think of all the things I have left to say,
all the questions he could have answered,
all the history he could have handed me,
all the ways we never got to relate,
but then Baba Joon starts to cry,
and then Baba Joon starts to shake,
and the fire in me starts to fade
as his tears wet my shoulder.

That's when I remember all the rest.
Baba Joon trying to teach us backgammon,
giving up, exploding, walking away,
ignoring me in the living room,
missing my *mehmooni* debut,
leaving Maman Joon,
leaving us all
behind.

I close my eyes — and I let go.
I turn around and walk back to Mom,
as she glares over my head
at her father
behind me.

Outside

We walk down the stairs.
It's still raining.
But that desert smell,
that freedom smell,
is back home
in Tucson.

Or at least,
I really hope it is.
Because it sure isn't here.

Mom reaches out and grabs my hand
and squeezes it tight, like a promise
that she would never leave me.

Neverland

Mom hails a cab and we get in.
The cabs in London are all black,
with rounded edges and protruding headlights
that look like eyes. Like the kind of cab you might see
in a cartoon, like in the opening sequence of *Peter Pan*,
before the kids leave London behind and fly off
to Neverland.

The seats inside are leather, like Mona's couch.
I think of Mona and Baba Joon, who are
probably sitting on that couch right now,
trying to figure out what just happened,
while the dead zebra wonders
who exactly I was and why
I left my tea unfinished.

But Baba Joon isn't talking to Mona on the couch.
He's standing outside. In the doorway, waving.

"Where to, miss?" the driver asks.
"Mom, look!" I said.

She sees Baba Joon and sighs, heavy.
My mom is so tired. She doesn't wave back.

But Baba Joon keeps waving.
And we lock eyes through the glass.
And for just the briefest moment,
his lips tighten, he tilts his head
the way he does when he has
something he has to say.

He wants to tell me something.

I want to hear what it is.

"Can I go?" I ask Mom.

"Yes, you can. Of course you can . . .
But be quick, joonam."

So I open the door,
look both ways,
and cross the street.

Never Forget

Baba Joon hugs me.
He is not crying anymore.
He just wants more time
to say goodbye.

After what feels like forever,
he leans back to look at me and says,
"Never forget where you came from, Omid jan."
And then he switches to English to say,

"I love you."

If there was
ever a time to *tarof*,
this, right here,
right now,
is it.

But I hesitate.

Because so much, too much, is already unclear.
Because I don't know how he could leave us like that.
Because I don't know why he's here, or why he didn't warn me.
But most of all, because I don't know
if this will be the last time
I speak to him.

Here's what I do know.
I know I wouldn't want the last thing
I say to Baba Joon to be in English.
I know that in my bones.

So, no, I can't say,
I won't say,
"I love you, too."

Instead, I switch to Farsi,
and tap into that feeling I had
rapping at the Globe, that feeling
of finding the right words, the right way.

I return to Farsi and use a phrase I remember from
back when I was a kid, back before all the English.

"Khaylee dooset daram."

He smiles
one of those broken smiles
that run in our family.
He kisses the top of my head.
Then he switches back to Farsi and says,

"Good, good, my sweet boy,
now go to your mom."

A Hard Thing To Say, Part 3

I love you
is ~~a hard~~ ~~harder~~
an impossible thing to say
if you're speaking Farsi.

Literally.

You can't say it.

Not the way you do in English.

I think it's because Persians are poets.
Not by choice, but by design,
by way of millions of mehmoonis
and songs that rhyme with prayer
and thousands of years of old stories
becoming new again, there's poetry
passed down, always
on the tip of the tongue.
And all this poetry has seeped
into the way we speak
to each other.

So when it comes to love,
it's go big or go home.

It's easy to confess your heart's affection to a soul mate,
to a perfect partner, to your one-in-a-million.
It's easy, in Farsi,
to exclaim,

"Asheghetam!"
                    which means
                                        "I am in love with you!"

But the actual word you use for "love," in that context,
doesn't work for family members. Not for brothers.
Or sisters. Or fathers. Or mothers. Or grandsons.
Or grandparents.

In those cases, you say,

"Khaylee dooset daram"
                    which means
                                        "I like you very much."

Then you just hope
the other person
understands.

Across The Divide

So I hoped
he would understand.
But I knew
he might not.
And for the first time
that was okay
with me.

Because I had said what I meant.

With no time to pretend or plot.
No script memorized.
No series of rhymes.
No safety net.

It was all me. Just me.

And I was happy.
Because words can be
so hard. I've been trying,
my whole life trying,
to use my words
to get people who exist outside of me
to understand something
that exists inside of me.

It doesn't always work.

And even when it does,
it's never easy.

But I have to keep trying —
we have to keep trying —
to pass that baton
across the divide.

Speaking,
any language,
is a compromise.
It's the reward of being heard
meets the risk of being misunderstood.

It's taking a shot at a connection . . .
and people miss the mark all the time.
But in that moment
with Baba Joon,
I didn't miss.

I know grandkids are supposed to love their grandparents.
I know I'm supposed to love Baba Joon. I know
I was on my way. I wanted to. I was trying to,
at his house, on the hike,
even in the dairy aisle.
But then — he just left.

He stopped trying.

So I never found out
if I can love Baba Joon.
All I know, after everything,
is that I like him
very much.

Which is *exactly* what I said.

Which means, in that moment,
Farsi, *my* Farsi,
was perfect.

In The Rear View

I got back in the car,
and the driver took off as soon as the door closed.
I watched as Baba Joon got smaller and smaller in the rear view.

Mom never looked back.
She never saw him disappear.

She made herself busy instead,
giving our driver the address of our Hilton,
making sure we were heading in the right direction.

I turned back around
and saw her
differently.

She was still my mom,
but I'd learned so much. She was my mom
who had once performed in plays,
and read poems at mehmoonis,
and has old friends
in London.

"I love you, Mom."
"I love you too, baby."

Brothers, Part 5

Back in the hotel room,
I asked Mom if I could dial Amir.

I wanted to tell him everything
about the London Bridge and the Globe Theatre,
and about Fariba letting me perform onstage,
and about Baba Joon and Mona, too.

I wanted to tell him the whole thing
felt like some kind of dream.

But as soon as he picked up the phone,
he had something he wanted to say.

"Omid! Guess what, dude!!!"
"Yo, what's up?"

"So . . . I talked to Mr. Thompson at school today . . .
and it's official! I'm taking over the part."
"Holy crap, are you for real?!"

"For real. I'm gonna play Bottom in *Midsummer*."
"Amir. Bro. I am so proud of you."

                                        I really was.

"I can't wait to do it!"
"I can't wait to see you do it."

                            And that was all that mattered.

The Too-Big Truth

We're heading home in the morning.

I should be sleeping.
Instead I'm thinking
about how the world
is getting smaller.

We've invented
phones and planes
to connect and carry us
from one side of the world
to the other side of the world
a thousand times faster
than our ancestors
could ever
imagine.

But the world is getting bigger too.

London used to be a word.
Just a word. A proper noun. Like New York, Paris,
Berlin, or Tehran. But now it's a proper place,
filled with fog and double-decker buses
and hotel rooms and black pudding
and blue paintings and blueprints
and Big Ben and Baba Joon,
and that still doesn't make sense, but it's true,
and I guess the truth won't always make sense
because it's just so big.
Too big.

Like you-can-never-wrap-your-arms-around-it-
no-matter-how-hard-you-try big.

And that's just London.

A few hours away from anywhere by plane.
Like New York, Paris, Berlin, or Tehran.
Each a proper place with its own piece
of the too-big truth
that I would like
to wrap my arms around —
even if my fingers
never touch.

Omid

"Flight attendants, please prepare the cabin for takeoff."
And just like that, we're up in the air again.

Mom tells me Baba Joon might not come back.
Mom tells me a story.

When Mom and her sister were younger
and had just moved to America,
her parents struggled.
Baba Joon and Maman Joon
did not live happily ever after
after their daughters left,
because some part of them
had left too.

Maman Joon turned to faith.
Baba Joon turned to friends.

One in particular.

Mona was Azadeh's best friend,
a young assistant architect,
who dreamed and built
new possibilities
for a world
that needed them,
for the people
who needed them.

Baba Joon dreamed of Mona.

Baba Joon needed Mona
in a way my mom could never forgive.

I see a reflection
of the past in the present
and I have to ask,
"Is that what's happening at home?
Are you and Dad — "
"No, Omid. No. That's not what's happening."

I am flying through the air.
Toward home,
the only one I've ever known
but am starting to see
differently.

I am flying through the air.
Toward a window.
And I don't know
if I'm a bird
or a rock.

And then we hit turbulence.

My body tenses as I grip my chair.
Mom sees me struggling. She says
it's normal. Tells me she actually
likes it when the plane
shakes a bit.
"That's ridiculous, Mom.
How — how is this normal?
It feels like we're falling."

"No," she says, "it feels
like being caught
over and over again."

She says something
    about trying to find
        the calm in commotion.

But I'm starting to sweat
    and can't imagine how
        anyone could do that.

She tries again to help me.
"Did I ever tell you the greatest gift your father ever gave me?"
"Nope," I say, surprised she's talking so casually,
that she isn't afraid in what feels like a storm.
"He asked me to choose your name."

That's not what I expected her to say.

"Of course, I returned the favor.
I asked him to choose your brother's name.
And he chose 'Amir.' Which means to be a prince. To rule.
Your baba is a good man.
Everyone needs something to hold on to
when the world is unpredictable and confusing.
Your dad's gift is that he chooses to make that thing
for himself, for those he loves; he creates the control
we all need. He sees the world as something to mold.
That's the gift he gives you boys.
You will make paths
where there are none.

But still, he let go of that control
when he asked *me* to name *you.*

The longer we lived in America,
the more distant I felt from my parents.
The longer I lived with your dad,
the more distant I felt from my sister.
But then you arrived. And you were everything
I ever wanted. And I knew, I could never feel
distant from you. Your dad and I cared
for each other, yes, but now we had you
to care for, too.
And no matter what happened,
we would do anything,
everything
to protect you.

Your Farsi used to be excellent, Omid,
but it's still good . . . better than you give it credit for.

Do you know what 'omidvaram' means?"

Better than I give it credit for.

"Doesn't it mean, to be — sure?"

Mom laughs. "Not quite, joonam, but I understand why
you'd think that. Sometimes people say it when
they want to be sure of something."

The plane stops shaking.
I let go of my chair, relieved,
but Mom keeps going,

like she needs me
to hear this part.

"'Omidvaram' means 'I am full of hope,'

or 'I hope.'

'Omid' means 'hope.'"

I remember how I felt
when I walked away
from Baba Joon.

How I was sad,
but for some reason,
I was hopeful too.

"Hope, Omid jan. Always, hope.
You are my hope.
You have shown me
that no matter how many
languages you must learn,
or how far away you are
from the people you love,
no matter how hard life gets —
good things
do happen."

Mom kisses my forehead,
then closes her eyes.

Hours pass.

I try to sleep but can't.
My body is tired, but
my mind is awake
and full of hows . . .

How I got here.

How the past is like a path,
or a hike, filled with people
who didn't quite know
which way to go.

How some stayed on the road together,
while others went off
on their own.

Thinking about Mom and Dad
and Maman Joon and Baba Joon in the past,
making decisions, making mistakes, makes me realize . . .
I'm going to be in the past one day too.
And I can't stop time from moving forward
or mistakes from being made —
so why be so afraid?

If our destiny is just one change of plans after another,
why put so much pressure on finding a perfect plan
in the first place?

And what is perfect, really?

Maybe it has nothing to do with other people's expectations.
Maybe it has to do with the moments I really feel — like me.

Maybe that's as close to perfect as we can be?
Maybe that's how I move forward.

I've felt "like me" before.
I know I can do it again.

I felt it being Bottom.
I felt it flying with Mom.
I felt it on the phone with Dad.
I felt it in Sammy's music and sometimes in Emily's too.
I felt it talking things through with Amir.
I felt it writing raps.

No one way of being can contain
all of me, just like no one language
can contain every thought, every feeling.

I know because I felt it with Baba Joon, too.
Saying goodbye in London.
I felt like me, in Farsi.
And I want to feel that more often.

"Mom?"

"Yes, joonam?"
"Do you think when we get home,
you and Dad could start
talking to me more
in Farsi?"

She smiles, bright.
Like the family curse
of the broken smile might

have just been banished
to some foreign land.

And then the turbulence hits us again.

Even harder than before.
This time the captain's voice
comes on over the in-flight intercom.
He sounds calm, like Mom.

"Forgive the bumpy air along the way, folks.
We're heading into our final descent
toward Tucson International Airport.
It's been a pleasure flying with you all.
Flight attendants, please prepare
the cabin for landing."

I close my eyes
and breathe in deep
and for just a moment —

I believe.

Everything
will be alright.

Omidvaram.

Acknowledgments

The women to whom this book is dedicated—Jessie Mahon, my wife; Parisa Arabshahi, my mom; and Rebecca Sherman, my agent—trusted my creative impulse and urged me to write long before I believed I could. There are no suitable words, only gratitude forever. Anne Hoppe, my editor, mentor, and friend, is a force of insight and generosity who took a chance on me and Omid and bettered our story in every imaginable way. Anne, you changed my life and made the impossible possible. *Dastet dard nakone.*

There are so many people who have helped me, who deserve my thanks and recognition.

Arteen Arabshahi, my brother; Majid Arabshahi, my dad; and my entire wonderful family for supporting my dreams and aspirations relentlessly, especially when I doubted them. PigPen Theatre Co., my dearest friends, fellow makers, and chosen family. If even a modicum of what I've learned from you (tone and character from Dan Weschler, subtlety and metaphor from Ryan Melia, humor and accountability from Ben Ferguson, levity and bravery from Curtis Gillen, consideration and commitment from Alex Falberg, structure and range from Matt Nuernberger) ended up in these pages, I'd consider myself one smart cookie.

Saks Afridi, the brilliant artist whose body of work inspired me to explore cultural fusion long before one of his stunning pieces graced the cover of this book. Francesca Mercurio, my therapist, whose thoughtful guidance and honesty over the years has made me a less reactive, more reflective, and wholly happier person. Phil Kaye, who was one of the first friends I spoke to about the ideas in this story and whose perspective was invaluable throughout the writing process. Daniel Nayeri, a generous friend and role model, whose presence in my life has made it better in ways I didn't know I needed. Arian Moayed, whose values, kindness, and—to get very specific—half-Farsi, half-English production of *Hamlet* featuring a cast of Persian actors inspired me endlessly. Melissa and David Cornell, who are incredible humans, first readers, and friends.

A few fellow writers, in no particular order. Jon Sands, Kae Tempest, Sarah Kay, Linda Sue Park, Jason Reynolds, Adib Khorram, Hanif Abdurraqib, Neda Maghbouleh, Nasir Jones, Mahogany L. Browne, Sharon Creech, Min Jin Lee, Talib Kweli, Kazuo Ishiguro, Adam Bradley, Alan Bennett, Lin-Manuel Miranda, Elizabeth Acevedo, and Marshall Mathers. Thank you for your words: they've had a lasting influence on mine.

Finally, you. Dear reader! YOU are the reason writers write. Not only did you read this book, but you're reading all these names too, which means you're curious, which is one of the best things any of us can be. Thank you for spending your precious time with me and this story.

I'm deeply grateful.

With love,
Arya